Kingdom Keepers

DISNEY IN SHADOW

BOOK THREE

RIDLEY PEARSON

Kingdom Keepers

DISNEY IN SHADOW

BOOK THREE

DISNEP • HYPERION

Los Angeles   New York

The following are some of the trademarks, registered marks, and service marks owned by Disney Enterprises, Inc.: Adventureland® Area, Audio-Animatronics® Figure, Big Thunder Mountain® Railroad, Disneyland®, Disney-MGM Studios, Disney's Animal Kingdom® Theme Park, Epcot®, Fantasyland® Area, FASTPASS® Service, Fort Wilderness, Frontierland® Area, Imagineering, Imagineers, "it's a small world"®, Magic Kingdom® Park, Main Street, U.S.A. Area, Mickey's Toontown®, monorail, New Orleans Square, Space Mountain® Attraction, Splash Mountain® Attraction, Tomorrowland® Area, Toontown®, Walt Disney World® Resort.

Buzz Lightyear Astro Blasters © Disney Enterprises, Inc./Pixar Animation Studios

Toy Story characters © Disney Enterprises, Inc./Pixar Animation Studios

Winnie the Pooh characters based on the "Winnie the Pooh" works by A. A. Milne and E. H. Shepard

Copyright © 2010 Page One, Inc.

Printed in the United States of America
First Hardcover Edition, April 2010.
First Paperback Edition, March 2011. 10 9 8 7 6 5 4 3 2
FAC-025438-18365
ISBN 978-1-368-04627-5

Visit www.disneybooks.com, www.thekingdomkeepers.com, and www.ridleypearson.com

SUSTAINABLE
FORESTRY
INITIATIVE

Certified Sourcing

www.sfiprogram.org
SFI-01054

The SFI label applies to the text stock

*The Kingdom Keepers series is dedicated to
Storey and Paige, for helping me see the world
through their eyes. . . .*

A NOTE FROM THE AUTHOR

A great deal can change over the years, especially at Walt Disney World: new technologies, new attractions, and whole worlds. As a Keeper of the Kingdom, I felt so much has changed that it was time to update my stories to reflect those changes. Sometimes I changed only the name of an attraction or the description of a waiting line, but I often rewrote chapters or even whole sections of a book. The fun of *that* is, you are holding a new and updated Kingdom Keepers novel. (And the first editions remain available for those who like things just the way they were.)

So join the Keepers and me on *new adventures inside Disney's new attractions,* but following the same important mission: to prevent the Overtakers from stealing the magic and ruining the fun. Disney after dark has never been so unexpected. Enjoy!

—*Ridley*

1

FINN WHITMAN RAN HARD, then all the harder still, Terry Maybeck by his side and keeping up. By day, Tom Sawyer Island in the Magic Kingdom was an intriguing tangle of trees and bushes interrupted by meandering pathways. By night, it was something altogether different.

Four insanely angry, sword-carrying pirates ran close behind the two boys. Behind them came an alien that looked part koala bear, part cuddly dog.

The pirates had leaped from the shadows outside of Pirates of the Caribbean. Stitch had no business in the Magic Kingdom, yet there he was.

Finn glanced back at the pirates.

"Don't look back!" Maybeck said sharply. "Our holograms are like flashlights. Our outlines glow, don't forget."

The boys weren't exactly boys. They were projections of boys. Hologram projections. Their real selves—their bodies—were home, asleep in bed. Disney had selected them to model as hologram Park guides. The Disney Hologram Interactive program—DHI—was an incredibly popular service. It was now available in all four Walt Disney World Parks. But something had gone wrong with the projection technology. (Or maybe someone had made it "go wrong.") Sometimes at night, when asleep, the five kids who'd become DHIs ended up transformed into the Parks as their holograms. They were still getting used to it.

Maybeck had no shortage of self-confidence. He considered himself better than most people at nearly everything. His great-great-grandparents had been slaves. His grandparents lived as sharecroppers on Florida sugarcane plantations. Maybeck was fiercely proud of his African American heritage. He was embarrassed however, even shamed, that his parents had abandoned him with an aunt. He'd been raised by his Aunt Jelly, whom he loved. But he tried too hard to seem perfect. It could be annoying.

Currently, the other three DHIs, Philby, Willa, and Charlene, were supposed to be awaiting the two boys. They had a hideaway in the Indian Village across the lagoon from Tom Sawyer Island.

The five DHIs had a problem. The Disney Legend and former Disney Imagineer, Wayne Kresky, was missing. Wayne had created the DHI program. The five DHIs—sometimes called the Kingdom Keepers—were determined to find him.

"You know the movie *Toy Story*?" Wayne had asked Finn. This was back during the first time Finn had gone to sleep only to "wake up" as his Disney hologram inside Magic Kingdom.

"Of course."

"Andy's toys come alive when he leaves the room."

"I know," Finn had said.

"Well, that wasn't exactly a new idea around here. Walt designed it so that when the last of the humans— the guests, the cast members, the cleaners, maintenance personnel, even the Security guys—leave the Magic Kingdom, the characters get to have the Parks all to themselves."

"That's impossible."

"I'm serious," Wayne had said. "We didn't know it. We took a long time to figure it out. We would find Audio-Animatronics in different positions than we'd left them. Strange, unexplainable stuff. We finally realized Walt had wanted it this way. So, we left things alone."

"And I'm supposed to believe this?"

"We believe what we want to believe, Finn."

"That Disney characters come alive at night inside the Parks?"

Wayne had been telling the truth. But it took Finn and his friends a long time to be convinced.

"I had a pet monkey when I was a child," Wayne had once told Finn. "My mother gave it to me for my thirteenth birthday."

"Fascinating."

"No need for sarcasm, Finn. Franklin—I called him Franklin—was a great pet. A real friend. But something strange happened. The more freedom I gave Franklin, the more freedom he wanted. If I tried to put him in his cage at night, he fought me. He couldn't give up his freedom.

"Well, the same thing has happened to the characters," he continued. "They enjoy having the Parks all to themselves at night. The Disney villains, especially. They have become a problem. A big problem. They want the dark magic to defeat Walt's magic. They want the Parks for themselves. No good characters. No guests. To take over the Parks and make them dark and evil. That's unacceptable. That's where you and the other DHIs come in."

"What?" Finn's voice tightened.

"You five are going to defeat the Overtakers, the villains who want to take over the Parks."

"I don't think so."

"You'll see."

Finn remembered that night. Recalled how he'd felt about losing the Disney Parks. It was something worth fighting for. It was something worth trying to understand.

But Wayne had the answers.

They had to find him.

This was their fifth night searching the Magic Kingdom. Now that he and Maybeck had been spotted by the pirates, they were in trouble. The Overtakers, under Maleficent's leadership, would do anything to stop the DHIs. Anything.

"Maybeck," Finn said, "keep low."

Of the five DHIs, Finn had the most control over his hologram. The projections were not stable. If the kids felt fear, the holograms weakened and the kids could be hurt.

Wayne had taught Finn how to separate himself from fear. By doing so, Finn—even when not a hologram—could make himself a pure projection. An "all-clear" hologram. It didn't last long, but it was kind of like having a superpower.

Now, as projections, Finn and Maybeck ran through palm trees, rocks, and bushes.

The pirates closed the distance. They were only a matter of yards behind them now.

Maybeck, the faster runner of the two, called back to Finn, "Right now we could use a plan."

"I have one," Finn said. "Do you?"

They continued running, Finn out of breath, Maybeck not winded at all.

"That would be no," Maybeck said.

"All right then."

"All right then, *what?*"

"We'll go with my plan," Finn said proudly. Finn suddenly felt a burning sensation on his arm.

"Dude," Maybeck said. "Your arm is like, gushing blood."

Finn had caught the tip of a pirate's sword. It was a nasty cut, but it wasn't gushing. Maybeck also liked to exaggerate.

Whoosh! Finn heard a sword slicing the air just behind him.

Maybeck dropped to his hands and knees. Three pirates tripped over him. He jumped to his feet and caught back up to Finn.

"Okay, here's my plan . . ." Finn said. "How are you at swimming underwater?"

2

At FIRST, FINN ASSUMED THE ALLIGATOR was a Disney prop. But then a flicker of doubt crossed his mind. *Tom Sawyer* was set in Missouri. Alligators lived in Florida.

The alligator was real!

Swimming underwater, glowing slightly, Finn's eyes were open. Maybeck swam on his left. The alligator's mouth was wide open. Coming right at them.

The alligator was huge. Its mouth had a thousand teeth.

Finn reached over, grabbed Maybeck by the hand, and pulled him lower. The alligator swam above them. It turned with a flick of its massive tail and came at them again.

Finn heard a splash. The pirates or Stitch had entered the water behind them. The alligator turned yet again. It too had heard the splash.

Finn and Maybeck scrambled up a muddy bank at the Native American village. They were out of breath and spitting river water. They faced a semicircle of teepees, a fake fire pit, and a number of costumed Native American figures going about daily chores.

A cry of terror sounded from across the water. A pirate was going to be fitted with a wooden peg leg. The alligator had satisfied its appetite.

"You're late," Philby said. Philby was a tech freak, a computer nerd. He looked more like a redheaded soccer player. As kids chosen to be DHI models, the Keepers were mostly "average" in their looks. All but Charlene, who was gorgeous. She stood just behind Philby in front of one of the teepees. Charlene looked more like a teenage Disney Channel star. She had blond hair and a cheerleader's body. She was smart, athletic, cautious, and curious. Girls at school called her "unfair."

"We were worried about you," Charlene said. She pointed across the river. "Looks like for good reason."

"Yeah," Finn said, "we were delayed."

"The pirates were waiting for us," Maybeck said. "Waiting to grab us. To trap us. They chased us onto Tom Sawyer Island. We barely made it off."

"Are you saying they knew you were coming?"

"Felt like that," Finn said. "I suppose an Overtaker must have spotted us in the Park. The pirates were alerted."

"Let's get out of here before they come back." Charlene had an unnaturally loud cheerleader's voice.

Willa approached from the teepee. She looked Native American or Asian with her hooded, inquisitive eyes. She wore her dark hair braided. She'd gone to sleep in cargo pants and a T-shirt that read: BITE ME. On the back of the shirt was a photo of a shark.

Once inside the nearest of the six teepees, the Kingdom Keepers vanished. Their projections were blocked. They were in projection shadow. Impressions in the sand showed where they were sitting. They could still touch, feel, talk, smell, and hear. They even left footprints in the teepee's sand floor.

Their voices rang out in the darkness. To anyone looking inside, it would have appeared that no one was there.

Philby remained outside as lookout.

"So, what now?" Willa asked. "We've looked for Wayne everywhere. We've spent five days. I don't think he's in the Magic Kingdom."

Charlene agreed with Willa.

"That was a trap tonight," Maybeck said. "It's not safe here for us. We shouldn't hang around MK anymore."

"I guess," Finn said, "we move on. There have been no Overtaker sightings reported in Animal Kingdom. Epcot has been active. I suggest we look for Wayne there."

"My parents will ground me if I get caught in bed and they know I'm crossed-over as a hologram," Willa said. "They don't like me doing this."

"Yeah, same here," Maybeck said. "My aunt is freaked Disney will take away the college fund."

All five of the kids had been promised free college for modeling as the DHIs.

"We can't give up on Wayne," Finn said.

"We just have to be more careful," Willa said.

"Psst!" Philby signaled from outside the teepee door. "We've got company." Philby stepped inside. He disappeared into projection shadow.

"Ouch!" Philby had sat down on top of Finn's legs.

Finn moved over.

"Not a peep," Philby whispered. "It's a lot of them!"

A moment later, the crunch of dry palm fronds and jungle leaves could be heard. The pirates talked between themselves.

"They probably gone and skedaddled," said a man's voice.

"Footprints!" called another man's voice.

A shudder passed through each of the Kingdom Keepers. They had gotten careless.

The voices grew louder. Closer. The pirates were following the footprints toward the teepee.

"Here," a low voice growled.

A face appeared inside the teepee's open door. The man had a scraggly beard. Dark brown moles and warts mixed with scars. The pirate stepped inside.

Finn scooped up two big fistfuls of sand. His heart pounded in his chest.

The pirate looked searchingly into the teepee. "Ain't no one here," he said.

"But them tracks go in and don't come back out," said another. "Don't make no sense."

"Them kids is cagey," offered a third voice. "Wouldn't trust them with my teeth."

"You ain't got no teeth," said the man in the doorway. "Come take a look yourself."

A second face appeared in the doorway. This man had long, greasy hair, a gold hoop earring in his right ear, and a left eyelid partly sewn shut. He smelled like bacon fat and fish guts.

He also stepped inside. "Them tracks don't make no sense." He looked up into the peak of the teepee, searching for the kids. "And them tracks don't lie. They're here somewhere."

He looked right at the invisible Finn.

"Maybe they done dug themselves down into the sand like a flounder."

"You mean a stone crab," said the first man.

"I mean a flounder, you landlubber. Or a ray. Point

is, they could be hiding 'neath the sand and we wouldn't knows it, now would we?"

Both pirates stood inside the teepee. One was close to Philby. The pirates used their bare feet to dig into the sand.

"How would they be breathing under the sand?" the gravel-voiced pirate asked.

"How should I know?" answered the one-eyed stink bomb.

"Now!" Finn shouted. He stood and threw both handfuls of sand directly into the faces of the two pirates.

The pirates cried out, covering their faces. Philby tripped one. Finn shouted for them to run. Once out of the teepees their images reappeared.

Startled by the kids appearing out of thin air, two other pirates were met with sand in their eyes. Charlene pushed them over as they staggered back.

The Kingdom Keepers rushed out of the teepee as a group. Finn slipped and fell.

Stitch stood over him. "You don't belong here," Stitch said. He showed his sharp teeth.

Maybeck knocked Stitch over. Finn jumped up.

The boys chased after the other DHIs, following a trail that led back to the Park.

The pirates were up now. They ran hard to catch the kids.

"Ready to return?" Finn called. He held what looked like a car fob in his hand. The Return, as they called it, canceled projection. It returned their consciousness to their sleeping selves.

The Kingdom Keepers reached out and held hands as they ran.

Finn had never tried the Return while running. They'd always just stood together as a group. He had no idea if it would work.

"One . . ." Finn counted aloud.

The pirates gained on them. The clanking of swords could be heard.

"Two . . ."

Whoosh! A sword blade passed frighteningly close to Finn's head.

"Three!"

He pushed the button. All the holograms disappeared at once.

3

Finn opened his eyes. It was the same as always: he could barely see. His bedroom was cloaked in darkness. The only light came from the colorful LEDs on his computer. Hanging from the ceiling was a glow-in-the-dark mobile of the solar system. He reached out and touched his face, pulled on his ear. He was human. The Return had worked. He'd crossed over and was whole again.

If the other Kingdom Keepers had not had the exact same dreams as Finn, he might have never believed any of this.

His left arm stung. It felt sticky with blood. He pushed back the sheets. If his mother saw blood, she would know he'd crossed-over as a DHI. After the trouble in both the Magic Kingdom and Animal Kingdom, that was strictly forbidden. He would be grounded for a month or more.

There was a blood smear on the sheet. He'd been cut by a pirate's sword. It wasn't a deep cut, but it was inches long and still bleeding a little.

He was wearing cargo shorts and a Rays T-shirt.

His clothes were wet. The sheets were damp.

He cleaned and closed the wound with two Band-Aids. He'd have to wash his clothes without his mother knowing. Impossible. He washed them in the shower. He wrung them out and hung them in his closet to dry.

While most adults would not, could not, fully believe any of the stories about the Kingdom Keepers, Finn's parents didn't want him sneaking out at night. They'd installed an alarm system. Finn hadn't been told the security code. It wasn't to keep criminals out. It was to keep Finn in. Having crossed over at 4:00 a.m., Finn set his alarm for ten minutes before his parents woke up. He climbed back into bed and slept soundly. When he woke, he hurried downstairs to wash the sheets.

His mother didn't look good in the morning. She looked kind of scary. Her brown hair was tangled. Her face was plain and pale. Her eyes didn't open all the way. She scratched at her collarbone, rubbed her eyes.

"What are you doing?"

"Laundry. Sorry if it's loud."

"You are doing laundry?" she asked. "What's going on, young man?" When his mother used "young man," it usually meant Finn was already in trouble.

"I'm sorry, Mom. I might have spilled some food in bed."

"Oh, Finn, we talked about that! You're not allowed to bring food into your room."

"I know. I'm sorry. I was famished."

"You eat like a horse. You ate a gigantic dinner!"

"Sorry."

"You know the rules."

"I really am sorry."

"No more. Okay? We've talked about this." She turned and left him.

Finn celebrated his small success. It wasn't easy trying to save Disney World from the Overtakers. Harder still being the son of disbelievers.

He rode his bike to school. Locked it up behind the gym where bikes were parked. He walked around the corner and spotted a woman on the sidewalk. She walked slowly, carrying a purse and a Disneyland 50th Anniversary Celebration tote over her shoulder.

Finn knew the tote bag was a serious collector's item. He could see a dozen pins attached to the tote. They would no doubt be collectibles. Finn could spot a Disney fan.

She was looking at him. Focused on him. It gave him the creeps. Now a few steps closer he realized he'd seen the same woman yesterday. After school, when kids were leaving.

Maybeck had spoken of a woman coming to his

aunt's pottery shop. She snooped around but never bought anything. She seemed more interested in Maybeck. Was this the same woman? Was she some kind of Kingdom Keepers stalker? *Eww!*

They were going to need bodyguards before long!

Finn hurried to the front doors. He looked back. The woman had turned around. She was walking away from the school.

What's with her? Was he supposed to tell someone? Or was it up to him to find out for himself?

4

FINN'S FRIENDS MADE FUN OF GIRLS. They worked to embarrass them, tease them, and yet couldn't stop talking about them.

He'd met Amanda because of the Kingdom Keepers. She and Jess were the kind of close friends that called themselves sisters. Jess dyed her hair all different colors. In Finn's opinion, Amanda, sometimes called Mandy, wasn't like other middle school girls. She talked like a high schooler. She dressed in Goodwill. For a long time she and Jess had lived in an abandoned church. Both girls were orphans. Both had been in foster homes. Both had special powers. Both had been in a boarding "school" in Baltimore that had been more like a prison.

Jess sometimes dreamed about the future. And what she dreamed ended up happening.

Amanda could move things by waving her arms.

Neither girl understood why they had "abilities." But they'd learned how to use them. They called themselves Fairlies. "As in, fairly human," Amanda had explained.

Recently, the girls had been caught by something called Family Services. Not exactly the police, Family

Services had put them into yet another foster home. It was run by a woman called Ms. Nash. They didn't like Ms. Nash.

Finn caught up to Amanda at her locker. She looked sad.

"What's going on?" Finn asked.

"Jess and I are being moved back to Baltimore with the other Fairlies."

"The boarding school?"

"Yep."

"No way!" Finn said.

"They can do whatever they want," she said. "We have no parents, no relatives to object. Never mind that we both like school here. Never mind that we have new friends here." She let her words hang for a second.

"There is no way they're sending you back."

"You want to bet? And don't even mention the word *fair* because Jess and I have this thing about *fair*. It's the worst of all four-letter words, along with *hope* and *trust*."

"*Trust* is five letters."

"I don't want to go back there. People get paid for kids in foster care. Did you know that? Jess and I make Ms. Nash money. She'll fight to keep us in her house.

"How'd it go last night?" Amanda asked, changing the subject.

Finn considered trying to explain their search

for Wayne. Their being chased by pirates. Instead, he rolled up his sleeve and showed her his cut. "Pirates," he said.

"Yikes!" she said.

"First comes love, then comes marriage . . ." The voice of Greg "Lousy" Luowski carried from down the hall.

"Then come morons," said Finn.

Luowski, roughly the size of a soda machine and probably just about as smart, stepped up to Finn. He had a crush on Amanda, which made Finn the enemy.

"Hi, Greg," Amanda said.

Luowski grunted. His form of conversation.

"Howdy, big guy," Finn said.

"Where you sitting at lunch?" Luowski asked Amanda. In his world Finn didn't exist at the moment.

"See? He likes you," Finn said.

Luowski blushed through his freckles.

"I'll look for you, Greg. I'll definitely say hi but I'm sitting with Finn."

Luowski could give these looks that felt like a punch in the face. Finn's nose hurt. Luowski walked off, making a point of standing taller than everyone else.

"What a knucklehead," Finn said.

"I don't lose any sleep over Greg," Amanda said.

Touching Finn's wound lightly, she said it looked nasty. Finn told her about having to lie to his mother about eating in bed. They both laughed.

The bell rang.

"Don't mess with Greg, okay?" she said. "You heard about Sammy?"

Sammy Cravitz had had his nose broken by Luowski. The whole school had heard about it. All except the teachers, apparently. Or maybe the teachers had heard about it but were as scared as everyone else of Greg Luowski.

Finn's ability to force his all-clear DHI was a definite advantage. If Luowski took a swing at a hologram, he wouldn't connect. Finn wouldn't feel it. Luowski might even lose his balance and fall over.

"We have a favor to ask," Finn said.

"We?"

He lowered his voice. "The Keepers."

"Okay."

"You know how we're not allowed to go into any of the Parks. Not without permission. Because they don't want our DHIs and our real selves being seen at the same time."

"Yeah, I know."

"So we're going into the Park this afternoon. But with hats and glasses and stuff for disguises. Philby heard that an abandoned truck was found near Epcot. We're thinking it might be a clue."

"For finding Wayne."

"Right."

"Count me in," she said.

"I haven't even asked yet."

"How dumb do you think I am?" she said. "You want to ask me and Jess to help you check things out. The more of us, the more of the Park we cover. No problem. Are we done here?"

"Seriously," he said.

"The bell rang."

"I know."

"What exactly are we looking for, Finn?" she asked, shutting her locker.

"Philby thinks that if Jess gets close to Wayne—"

"She might 'see' something. It doesn't work like that. You know that. But maybe the temperature drops," Amanda said. "That would mean Maleficent is nearby. And maybe that leads us to Wayne."

"Who knows? That's what Philby thinks. The place is gigantic. That's all. We'll meet up and follow a plan. If you two help, it'll speed things up. Maybe we can narrow down an area to search once we cross over."

"You're really weird. You know?"

Finn didn't comment.

"Good weird," she said. "But weird. Check your e-mail." Neither she nor Jess had cell phones like the rest of them. "We'll go after school. I'll let you know if we find anything."

Good weird, Finn was replaying in his head.

He hardly heard the rest of it.

There was Greg Luowski staring him down from the hall.

Finn knew trouble was coming. That kid smelled of it.

5

AFTER SCHOOL, FINN GRABBED a baseball cap from his locker and donned a pair of shades on his way out of school. He biked to a bus stop, locked up, and rode the twenty minutes out to Walt Disney World. Soon, he was approaching the Epcot entrance. He didn't want to use his Magical Memories Pass to enter. It would alert the computer system that he'd entered the Park without permission. But Wayne had provided Finn and the other Kingdom Keepers fake employee passes during their search for Jess in Animal Kingdom. He tried that, and it worked.

He knew that Amanda had P.E. last period on Tuesdays, which meant she would be late. He definitely had a head start on her and Jess. Five minutes passed. Ten. It was dizzying trying to study the faces of the hundreds of people entering the Park in order to spot Amanda or Jess. When he freaked, it wasn't because he saw either of them. Instead, it was a woman. An adult.

The woman.

He'd only seen her from a distance at school. But he knew it was the same person.

Suddenly he felt pulled toward the entrance. He saw Amanda and Jess coming toward him.

Had the mystery woman's entrance been planned? Was she keeping watch on the girls?

"Hey!" Finn called out softly as Amanda and Jess approached.

They pretended not to hear. They continued walking and talking.

Finn kept his face lowered as he hurried to catch up. This was not a time to be recognized by a DHI fan.

Coming up from behind, he called out, "Psst! Amanda!"

She spun around. "Give us a minute."

Finn walked behind them. He waited. Amanda looked back. Finn caught up. "Hey, Jess."

"Hey, Finn."

Jess was a pretty girl. She looked a little bit like he imagined a fairy or maybe a good witch. Although she dyed her hair dark, its natural color was a shocking white. It had turned that color after Finn had rescued her from the clutches of a spell cast by Maleficent. For the past month she had been a strawberry blonde.

"You're not supposed to come here, right? You being

a celebrity and all," Jess said. She sounded half asleep. Super calm.

"You two are doing me and Wayne and all of us a favor," Finn said. "I waited around for you because I couldn't let you go it alone."

"So, it isn't that you wanted to hang out with Amanda?" Jess said a little hopefully.

"Jessica!" Amanda snapped, blushing.

"I wanted to hang out with both of you," Finn answered.

"And protect us, I suppose?" Amanda said.

"It's not like that," he said.

"No, it's not," Amanda said, "because if anyone recognizes you—and they are bound to because that disguise is . . . pitiful—then you mess us up a lot more than if we were just on our own."

"So you want me to leave?" he said.

"No," Jess answered, stealing the moment from Amanda. "She wants to pretend she isn't thrilled that you took a very big chance by coming here to protect us, and she wants to make it seem like it's no big deal. I like that there are three of us. I feel better that you're here. So does Amanda, though she'll never admit it."

"I don't have to admit what isn't true," Amanda said.

"There's a lot of Park to cover," Jess said. "Three people are better than two."

"It may be more complicated than that," Finn said. He led them behind a stand selling all kinds of merchandise. "There's this woman," he said. "She entered the Park right when you did. I think I saw her in front of school this morning. Maybeck said some woman was lurking around Crazy Glaze too."

"And she's here?" Jess said.

Finn nodded.

"So what do we do about it?" Jess asked.

Amanda lifted onto her toes to see over the stand, but Finn pulled her back down.

"I think I keep an eye on the woman, while you two search around for a temperature drop."

"We don't have phones," Amanda reminded him. "So what good does your following the woman do?"

"If she follows you two, we know we have trouble. If that happens, she is probably an Overtaker. And maybe if I can then follow her, she'll lead me to Wayne."

"You're dreaming," Amanda said.

"That's brilliant!" Jess said.

"And what if she's following you," Amanda asked. "What if her being here is a trap? How does that help anyone?"

Amanda's concern wasn't only about Finn. If she and Jess were caught, they'd probably be sent back to Maryland all the sooner.

"I say we call for a vote," Jess proposed. "All in favor of Finn following the mystery woman?"

Jess and Finn sheepishly raised their hands. "Whatever," Amanda said. "But if anything happens, you'd better leave us some clues. This Park is too big. We're not leaving here without you."

Finn nodded. "Sounds good to me."

"And me, too," Jess said.

Finn spotted a bright green balloon tied to a discarded stroller. "Keep a lookout," Finn said, "for that green balloon. I'm going to carry it low unless there's trouble. If you see a green balloon following you, it's me. It means something is wrong. So, if you see it, you'd better split up. No matter what, we all meet back here near the entrance in two hours so I can get home by dinner. Agreed?"

"I suppose," Amanda said.

"You're good at this," Jess said.

"I've had a little practice," Finn said.

The green balloon's ribbon in hand, Finn hurried off to catch up with the mystery woman.

6

"YOU WERE A LITTLE HARD ON HIM, don't you think?" Jess asked Amanda. They were headed toward The Land. Not only was Soarin' their favorite attraction in Epcot, but The Land offered a controlled environment— a cooler environment—and because of that, it seemed a good place to start in their search for the kind of cold Maleficent needed.

"I was only messing with him," Amanda said.

"He's worried about us."

"Yeah, right. But who's always getting into trouble?"

"We've had our share, too," Jess said.

Neither of them could forget the nightmare of Jess's being captured by the Overtakers. Finn had found her. Jess nearly reminded Amanda of that but knew she didn't need to.

"He's handy to have around at times like this," Jess said.

"I suppose. But it's risky for him—for all of the Keepers. I think it's stupid of him to come."

"You're worried about him! Do you have a crush on him or what?" Jess said.

"As if! You're the one he can't keep his eyes off. Him and every other boy."

"That is so not true!"

"We both know it is," Amanda said. "Hey, I'm good with it, so don't fight it." She lowered her voice. "Why do you keep checking your watch? We've got plenty of time before we have to be back."

"It isn't that," Jess said. "My watch shows the temperature. Elevation. A bunch of stuff. It's like for rock climbers and campers."

Amanda moved closer trying to see the watch face. "And?" she asked.

"No change so far. Eighty-two degrees."

"As in, boiling."

"Yeah, but my watch may pick up a change before we feel something."

The Land was housed in an inelegant glass-and-concrete dome. As the girls approached it, they walked slowly, trying to sense any change in temperature. Jess monitored her watch carefully.

"Nothing but hot," Jess said.

"Personally, I think this is hopeless," Amanda said. "I mean I know Finn and those guys felt a chill before, but give me a break."

"Any other ideas?"

"No."

Jess stopped abruptly.

"Jess?" Amanda said.

Jess just stood there.

"Hang on! I don't want to lose it," Jess said.

Amanda resisted saying something. Jess had a rare ability to dream things. But she'd never blanked out like this before. Amanda took Jess gently by the arm and steered her toward a concrete bench.

"Pencil," Jess said. She sounded sleepy. "I need something to write on."

Amanda dug through her purse. No pen, no paper, but she found some mascara. She slipped Jess's purse off her shoulder and rifled through it as well. She came up with a Winn-Dixie receipt. She put the mascara brush into Jess's right hand and the receipt onto her leg and steered Jess's hand to the receipt.

"Okay." She spoke softly.

Jess had that faraway look going. But her hand started moving. The mascara brush smeared black onto the receipt. It was no good: her effort was illegible. Amanda frantically dug through Jess's purse. In a zippered pocket she found a stumpy wooden pencil. She replaced the mascara with the pencil. Jess's hand began to scribble again.

She shaded and crosshatched, making the receipt darker. It looked like tall grass.

Amanda felt something weird and looked up.

She spotted a green balloon coming toward her. It was above the heads of the guests.

Finn's warning sign? She had to get Jess off the bench.

"We've got to get going," Amanda told Jess. "Trouble. We can't stay here."

Jess looked over at Amanda, then took in her surroundings. "Whoa," she gasped. She looked down at the receipt as if seeing it for the first time. "What's happening?"

"Come on! Now!" Amanda said. She grabbed the pencil and receipt. She stuffed them into her pocket.

The green balloon was closer, moving fast. It had to be Finn, and that meant trouble.

She and Jess moved toward The Land.

"It was like . . . one of my dreams," Jess explained. "You know? I was in the zone. But a daydream, not a night dream."

"You were definitely gone," Amanda said.

"It's never happened to me exactly like that."

Amanda glanced back. She saw a woman coming toward them. The woman had her hair up and looked more fancy than typical Park guests. Amanda knew immediately it was the woman. Finn's woman.

"It's her," she told Jess in a hush. "Stay with me."

Amanda picked up the pace. She and Jess entered The Land pavilion. The escalator was clear around on the other side. They hurried along the walkway that curved around the building. They could see down into the lower plaza. Small hot-air balloons hung from the ceiling. Colorful streamers cascaded down on all sides.

She avoided the pileup at the escalator and took the stairs, careful not to run and draw further attention.

Below them she saw a sea of cafeteria tables.

"This way!" she whispered. They reached the ground floor. Amanda looked up and spotted the green balloon only a few feet behind the woman.

Amanda dodged a few tables in order to hide from the woman.

Jess seemed dazed, like she'd just woken up.

Amanda considered heading into the women's bathroom, but they'd only trap themselves.

Jess pointed toward the waiting line for Living with the Land. "Other girls," she said.

It was a girls' volleyball or basketball team, by the look of them.

Amanda and Jess headed in that direction.

"I don't know," Amanda said. "We don't want to get stuck on a ride."

Jess ignored her. "Excuse me," Jess said. She pulled Amanda with her. They stood between two tall girls.

There was no way the woman would see them. Amanda kept watch for the green balloon but the girls around them formed a wall.

"Finn had better be careful," Amanda said.

"Yeah," Jess said.

The line surged.

The green balloon suddenly appeared. Both girls saw it.

Finn was somewhere behind them in the line.

"We'll be on the ride in less than a minute. What's the woman going to do then?"

"No idea," Amanda answered, "but I don't think I want to find out."

Some of the volleyball team boarded the two back rows of the nearest boat. This left the front three benches open. Amanda and Jess stepped into the front of the boat on wobbly legs. The green balloon had stopped moving. Finn was allowing others to pass him.

Looking back, Amanda spotted the well-dressed woman boarding two rows behind.

Amanda whispered, "She's behind us. What do we do now?"

Jess stared straight ahead.

"You got us into this," Amanda complained.

"I'm working on a plan."

"You don't have a plan?"

"I said I'm working on one! Give me a second."

A recorded voice warned visitors to remain seated and to stay inside the boat at all times."

"That's it!" Jess said, hearing the announcement.

Amanda turned sharply, looking in all directions. "Where? What?"

"I've got this. Do exactly as I say," Jess instructed.

"Really? That's what you've got?" Amanda sounded terrified.

The recorded voice warned of a storm. A brief explanation of the biodiversity of the planet followed.

"The American prairie once appeared as desolate as the desert," the voice continued.

"Get ready," Jess hissed.

"For what?"

"Trust me."

"Psst! Girls?"

Jess and Amanda froze. The voice was close behind them. A woman's voice. The woman's voice.

"I need to talk to you. It's about—"

"Shh!" One of the volleyball players interrupted the woman.

The boat entered a dark tunnel. Video screens showed working farms, insects and tractors.

"Get ready to jump," Jess whispered.

"What?" Amanda whined.

"Now!" Jess said, taking Amanda's hand. The two girls hopped off the boat onto a walkway. Jess pulled Amanda down with her, trying to hide in the low light of the tunnel. An alarm sounded. The boats stopped. Everyone was talking at once: "They got off! . . . I saw that! . . . You can't do that!"

Amanda and Jess had tripped the ride's emergency stop. "Let's go!" Jess hissed, pulling Amanda with her.

The girls hurried to the end of the tunnel. They were inside a greenhouse where banana and other fruit trees rose out of sand.

Two men in coveralls, working on some plants, turned and shouted, "Hey, you! Stop! You can't get out of the boats!"

"My sister can't hold it in another minute," Jess said. "Mexican food, you know?"

"Oh . . . thanks," Amanda hissed at Jess.

"Doesn't matter. You can't get off the boat like that."

"Mister, my sister got to get to the girls' room right now!"

The alarm stopped. The boats started moving again.

"Your tickets will be pulled," the worker said.

"Please! This is an emergency!" Jess called back.

"There's a lavatory down there." The worker pointed.

Jess elbowed Amanda. "Huh?" Amanda said.

"The girls' room," Jess said emphatically.

"Oh, yeah," Amanda said, "right." She headed in the direction the man was pointing.

Behind her, two men in lab coats arrived through a door and moved toward Jess.

Amanda hoped they weren't Overtakers.

7

WITH HER ARMS CROSSED, Ms. Nash looked scornfully at Jess and Amanda.

Ms. Nash clearly ate well, had no love of makeup or hairdressers, and thought of the Salvation Army as her go-to fashion choice. Her arms showed reddish patches of dried skin.

"What exactly were you thinking?" she wheezed.

Ms. Nash had trouble breathing.

"Amanda had to go. You know, to the bathroom," Jess said. "Number two."

"Never mind that! We have an understanding. The Disney Parks are off limits. Those friends of yours are off limits. They bring you nothing but trouble. And here we are again." Ms. Nash—the girls called her Ms. Rash—had been assigned by the State of Florida to take care of the two, an entirely one-sided agreement. "After everything that happened to you, Jessica, I'm surprised you'd get anywhere near that place."

"I love Disney World," Jess said softly. "Especially Epcot. We just wanted to have some fun."

"Life is more than fun. Did you also plan on missing dinner and curfew? You know how much a wasted dinner costs?"

For Ms. Nash, everything came down to dollars. Every month the state mailed her a check based on the number of girls she looked after. If Amanda and Jess were sent back to the Baltimore boarding school and removed from her care, her monthly payment would be less.

There was a stomping upstairs that won her attention and distracted her. Seven other foster girls lived in the house along with Jess and Amanda. Three bedrooms, one bath. A washing machine, no dryer. Making any kind of noise was against the rules. Ms. Nash had apparently been born strict.

"We didn't mean to miss dinner," Jess said apologetically. "The meals here are so . . . wonderful." Disgusting boiled meat and canned vegetables was the truth.

"There's no need for sarcasm, young lady."

"Yes, Ms. Nash."

"You're both grounded for two weeks. Do you understand me? Directly from school to this front door. 'Do not pass Go. Do not collect two hundred dollars.' Are we clear?"

"Yes, Ms. Nash," both girls said, nearly in unison.

"Your behavior reflects poorly on this house and my ability to care for you and the other girls. I hope you'll consider that the next time you think about doing something as foolish as what you've done."

"Yes, Ms. Nash."

"Up to your room," she said. "You will do your homework. You missed dinner. That's your problem."

"Yes, Ms. Nash." Again, nearly in unison.

The woman eyed the girls suspiciously. She appeared to understand they were mocking her. But she wasn't sure how to react.

"Well? What are you waiting for?"

The girls headed for the stairs. Suzie Gorman and Patricia Nibs had been spying on them from the stairwell. The two took off upstairs as Amanda and Jess approached. Upon being assigned to the Nash House, Amanda and Jess had been teased by the other girls. Eventually, Amanda and Jess found a way to keep their distance and maintain a truce.

There were no doors on any of the three bedrooms. No real privacy. Jess and Amanda sat side by side on Jess's lower bunk bed. They pulled out their homework and went to work. There were no desks or bookshelves in the small room, just three beds—a bunk bed and a twin-size roller bed—and a shared clothes dresser. Amanda started in on her math assignment. Jess had her diary open in her lap. The wrinkled, mascara-stained receipt was unfolded next to it. The pencil sketch, too.

"What's up?" Amanda said.

"It was like in one of my dreams. My nightmares, where I see the future. You know?"

"But outside The Land this time, and during the day."

"Yeah. But I didn't get all of it. It was more like a phone call where the person hangs up."

She sketched in her diary.

Amanda watched as the drawing took shape. A wall of tall grass. A chair.

It looked like a torn photograph. Part of the picture was there. Part was missing. The grass looked more like tall weeds. It was hard to tell what it was.

"Do you remember it?" Amanda asked.

"Not all of it, no. But what I do remember is pretty clear. Like the rest of them."

"And you think it's important?"

"It has never happened to me like that: during the day, in the middle of everything. It's always at night when I'm dreaming. It's always when I wake up and I can't get it out of my head. But today, in the Park . . . it just hit me all of a sudden. Like you'd put a bag over my head or something. Like I'd walked into a movie theater. Yeah, more like that. Only now I can't remember exactly what I saw. All I know is that it scared me, whatever it was. I didn't like it. I didn't want to see it. Most of the time, you know, it doesn't feel like that. I don't really care one way or the other—it's just sort of there, like that glow in your eyes after a camera's flash. Like that."

"So you think it means something?"

"It must," Jess said, nodding. "I mean it seems like they all mean something. And this one . . . this one was different."

An hour later they'd made it through their homework. They hurried to get in line for the bathroom so they could take showers before bedtime. An hour later they were in their beds reading. Amanda leaned over the edge of her upper bunk. "I wish we could have talked to him," she said.

"*Shh!*" hissed Jeannie Pucket from the rollaway. Jeannie made a point of being obnoxious whenever possible. She was Ms. Nash's favorite and, as a result, got all sorts of privileges the other girls did not. Amanda suspected she was also a spy for Ms. Nash, so she hadn't mentioned Finn by name.

"He figured it out," Jess said. "He's smart that way."

"But still."

"I'll see him tomorrow at school. You'll see. I'm sure he's worried about us. He won't be mad."

Ms. Nash didn't allow the girls to take phone calls.

"Be quiet," Jeannie said. "I'm trying to read."

Amanda groaned and lay back in her bed. Not long after that, the lights were turned off. Ms. Nash patrolled outside the rooms. Amanda fell into a troubled but deep sleep.

Sometime in the middle of the night, the bunk shook. Amanda emerged from a strange dream that involved Finn. She opened her eyes. A shadow moved on the opposite wall. Jess's reading light from the bottom bunk. Amanda hung her head over the side.

Jess was sketching in her "dream diary."

"You okay?" Amanda whispered, trying to keep from waking Jeannie.

"Fine. Go back to sleep."

"It's late."

Jess told her she'd had the same dream as earlier.

"The one in the Park?"

"That's the one."

Amanda strained to try to see the sketch. Jess moved the diary to prevent its being seen.

"I'll show you when I'm ready," Jess said.

Amanda climbed into Jess's bed. She slipped under the covers.

"How about now?"

Jess lowered the cloth diary, the page open to her sketch.

"Is that . . . Wayne?" Amanda asked.

"I think so. Yes."

"What's that behind him?"

"Grass? I'm not sure. But it's basically the same thing I saw this afternoon."

The image was of an old man sitting in a chair. A wall behind him with some grass on it.

"So you dreamed this twice today. Both times nearly the exact same thing?"

When Jess's dreams repeated, they came true at some point in the future. They both knew it. It had happened so many times. Amanda said, "I know this sounds stupid, but do you think Wayne is trying to send you a message?"

"No idea. Who knows?" Jess started drawing. She added shading to the back wall. It almost looked like a huge window.

"We've got to show this to Finn," Amanda said. "Maybe he's seen someplace like it in person."

Jess continued sketching. She drew dark circles beneath Wayne's eyes.

"He's in trouble," Jess whispered.

"Maybe we all are," said Amanda.

8

I<small>F</small> F<small>INN</small> <small>HAD</small> <small>RIDDEN</small> <small>HIS</small> <small>BIKE</small> straight home instead of stopping at the school's skate park, things might have ended up differently. He blamed Amanda. Once she showed up, he didn't feel like leaving.

She came running up to him, red-faced and out of breath. "Oh, good. I thought I'd missed you."

"Here I am."

"You most definitely are."

She reached into her backpack. "I have something to show you."

"I kinda need to get home," he said.

"Oh, no," she said, looking past Finn

Lousy Luowski was coming toward them. Flanked by Mike Horton and Eric Kreuter, Luowski had the face of an angry Rottweiler. The other two boys tried hard to act tough, but Luowski was the troublemaker.

Amanda held a small notebook in her hand. The title, *My Dreams*, was written in Sharpie. Finn knew exactly what it was. He wanted a look at Jess's dream book.

"You and me . . . we're going to fight," Lousy said.

"You're kidding, right?" Finn said.

"Do I look like I'm kidding?"

"That's original."

Lousy Luowski smelled like the laundry bin in the school locker room. He had a string of zits stretching from his nose toward his left ear. Hairs stuck out from the zits like stubby antennas.

Finn struggled to look calm. Dogs could sense when one was afraid.

"Hey, Greg, I can talk to a friend if I want to," said Amanda.

"Him and me, we've got some business to settle," said Luowski.

"Spoken like a true diplomat," said Finn.

Amanda shot Finn a look. It told him not to provoke Luowski. You don't tease a Rottweiler.

"Why don't we take it off school grounds?" Luowski said.

"Because," Finn answered, "if we take it off school grounds you will beat the snot out of me. I'm smarter than that. I'm smarter than you, Luowski. If we stay here, at least you'll get expelled. That might be worth the beating."

"You gotta go home sometime," said Luowski.

It was true. It would be easy enough for Luowski to wait him out. But Luowski didn't strike Finn as the patient type. Spontaneous violence was more like it.

"So," Luowski said, "whadda we got here?" He snatched the diary from Amanda's hand and waved it over his head tauntingly.

Finn lurched forward. Banging into Luowski was like hitting a steel post. "That's private property," Finn said.

"As if I care," Luowski said.

"You just stole a girl's private property. How do you think that'll go down, Greg?" Finn said. He reminded himself of his ability to briefly cross over into a DHI. Yes, it didn't last long. Yes, it made him tired. But at times it was valuable. Finn had promised Wayne not to do it. Wayne said it was dangerous to the DHI program. But Finn's father said there were exceptions to everything.

Friendship first. Finn's friendship with Amanda demanded he get back Jess's diary. He'd deal with breaking promises later. Luowski had no right to read Jess's diary. To so much as look at it.

Finn sought an inner quiet. It felt like he was slowing down time. His skin tingled. He felt like he was floating. He was overcome by dark. He saw the pinprick of light at the end of a tunnel. He crossed over.

He charged Luowski and snatched the diary. As Finn threw the diary to Amanda, Luowski took a swing at Finn. The boy's clenched fist punched through Finn's ghostly shoulder, hitting nothing.

Luowski lost his balance, having put his weight behind the blow.

"Run!" Finn shouted.

Amanda took off, the diary in hand. A confused Luowski planted his feet and delivered a second blow. Finn's body was still tingling—he was still crossed over. Luowski's knuckles passed through Finn's face and head. Again, Luowski lost his balance, believing Finn had somehow ducked the punch. Anger rose in Luowski's cheeks. Mike Horton would swear later he'd never seen someone move as fast as Finn had. Eric Kreuter would claim that Luowski hit Finn squarely in the jaw, but that nothing had happened.

With Luowski off balance, Finn jumped onto his bike and pedaled like a madman.

"Get on!" he called to Amanda as he caught up to her.

Amanda grabbed around Finn's waist. The bike wobbled and then sped away.

Luowski exploded with a string of curse words.

Amanda held more tightly as Finn took a turn. "Did you just—? Did I just see y—? What was that, exactly?" She sounded both excited and afraid.

Finn pedaled all the harder, desperate to get away from her questions.

9

Finn studied the page in Jess's diary. A buzz of conversation swirled around him and Amanda.

The Frozen Marble ice cream shop enjoyed a rush of middle school students each afternoon. Their table was near the back. Finn kept one eye on the front door in case Luowski had followed them.

Finn had sent a group text to the other Kingdom Keepers. He'd dropped a pin. Philby had the farthest distance to travel. He wouldn't make it. But Charlene and Maybeck might show up.

To Finn's complete surprise Philby was the first to arrive. He wore a ball cap pulled down tightly to hide his face, as did Finn. Being a Disney Park celebrity had gone from exciting to annoying. Neither of the boys wanted to spend time signing autographs and taking selfies.

"Hey." Philby pulled a chair up next to Amanda.

"Hey, yourself," said Amanda.

Finn felt like he wasn't at the table. He didn't like that. He slid Jess's open diary over to Philby. At the same moment Jess entered the shop.

"We can't stay long," Jess told Amanda. She turned to Finn. "In case you haven't heard, Ms. Nash grounded us."

Jess looked intensely at Finn. It felt to him more like she was looking through him or reading his mind. Truth be told, Finn was partly afraid of Jess.

"You drew that," Finn said, pointing to the diary in front of Philby. "And you and Amanda got in trouble with Park Security."

Philby's head snapped up.

As Jess was about to speak, Maybeck, Charlene, and Willa all entered the shop. Maybeck ordered a double scoop of vanilla mixed with peaches and almond crunch. That forced everyone else to order something. A few minutes later, the group sat in a circle around the two café tables eating ice cream.

Amanda spoke between mouthfuls. She told them about the trouble at Living with the Land. Jess then described both her daytime "nightmare" and the same dream waking her up the night before.

"Wayne's talking to her," Amanda said. "I know that's ridiculous, but it has to be."

Philby agreed with her.

"Let's say that's possible, not that I believe it." Of all of them, Maybeck struggled the most with the concept of magic. "What are we supposed to do about it?"

"We help find Wayne," said Charlene. All eyes fell on her.

Willa addressed Charlene, "I know you're a rally girl. A cheerleading champion and all. But I didn't think you liked trouble."

"I've changed," Charlene said.

"You think?" said Willa.

"The stilts," Charlene said. "Everything we did at Animal Kingdom. I can do stuff to help. I want to."

"You always help!" Willa said.

"But I've been feeling like I haven't been," Charlene said. "Look, I know that Disney hired me for my looks. All-American girl. Blond hair, blue eyes. A good bod. I get it. I always feel the rest of you are smarter than I am." She looked directly at Philby, then Willa. Switching to Maybeck, she said, "Or more creative. I didn't see where I fit into that. But Animal Kingdom changed it all. I can walk on stilts or climb walls. I'm athletic. I needed to figure out I had a place with the rest of you. If we're trying to rescue Wayne, I can help with that."

For a moment no one said anything. "Alrighty then," Willa said, breaking the ice. "So how 'bout we find Wayne?"

Maybeck had the diary in front of him. "Sorry to throw shade, but this drawing doesn't exactly tell us where he is."

"Check out his jacket," said Finn.

Maybeck leaned in close to the page. "You're kidding me, right?"

"It looks like a shield," Willa said, leaning into Maybeck.

"It's an EC shield," Finn said. "An Epcot Center windbreaker."

"So?" Maybeck didn't sound convinced. "Just because he's wearing Epcot merch doesn't mean he's in Epcot."

"Check out the stuff behind him," Finn said.

"Grass," Maybeck said. He turned to Jess. "Is that what it is? Grass?"

"I don't know," she said. "I just draw what I see."

"Note to Finn," Maybeck said, "tall grass is not exactly rare in Florida."

"It's not grass, and it's not a weed," Finn said. "And there's a reason it's blurry. A reason Jess drew it blurry."

"I hope you're going to share with the group," Maybeck said.

"If someone else figures it out, then I won't sound so crazy," Finn said.

"Here." Philby pulled the diary back in front of himself. Willa leaned in his direction. Charlene stood out of her chair and looked over Willa's shoulder.

"I know what it is," Willa said. "Hypothetically speaking."

"So, you're guessing," Maybeck said. "You're just trying to help Finn."

"Tell us!" Philby said.

"It's seaweed," Charlene said. "Kelp. It grows off the seafloor. Remember that scene when Harry Potter eats gillyweed? Kelp grows like a forest."

"So Jess was dreaming about a Harry Potter movie?" Maybeck could be a real tool sometimes.

"An aquarium," Willa said.

"Nemo and Friends," Philby said. "Eight thousand sea creatures, five million gallons of seawater."

"Wayne is underwater?" Maybeck snapped.

"There's a VIP suite upstairs, same as most of the other original pavilions. Probably hasn't been used for a long time, unless you count kidnapping a former Imagineer."

"We have to start somewhere, right?" Charlene said. "We can at least check it out."

"It's Jess's drawing. We need her and Amanda with us," Finn said.

"Are you saying what I think you're saying?" Amanda asked.

Philby caught on. "Because it'll be next to impossible to get a look at the VIP lounge the way we are. But if we were holograms, DHIs, then what's to stop us? We can walk through fences. We can walk through walls."

"How does that involve us?" Jess said. "We aren't Kingdom Keepers. We aren't DHIs."

"That's what Finn is saying," Charlene told Jess.

Willa said, "Finn wants Philby to mess with the DHI computer. He wants to turn you and Amanda into holograms."

10

THE MAGIC KINGDOM WOULD BE closing soon. Finn went to bed dressed in street clothes, including running shoes. So did Philby, Maybeck, Willa, and Charlene. If their parents and guardians had checked with one another, they would have stopped the Kingdom Keepers from crossing over as DHIs. Instead, Finn said good night to his parents, closed his bedroom door, and climbed between the sheets.

If he tried to sleep, he only prolonged his wakefulness. Philby had given him a book on self-hypnosis. It outlined a series of relaxation techniques, including reading something dry and challenging. Charlene had given every Kingdom Keeper a copy of *A New History of the Roman Empire*, a book so boring that it worked every time.

Maybeck used music. Charlene (despite her gift of the book), yoga. To each their own.

Somewhere around Rome's twelve bronze tablets Finn fell asleep. The only way he was certain of that was because he woke up.

In Disney World.

11

As FINN SAT UP, the air still smelled like fireworks. He looked over a low concrete retaining wall. There, a life-size bronze statue of Mickey Mouse was holding hands with Walt Disney. He knew exactly where he was.

Cinderella Castle rose a rich blue from the black asphalt. The castle spires stabbed the night sky. He felt a connection to this place. He loved the Magic Kingdom. It would always be a part of him.

"Fancy meeting you here." Maybeck walked toward Finn in dark clothing that would blend in with the night. He looked super cool, something that annoyed Finn. Maybeck couldn't help himself—he was the kind of guy who didn't ever try for cool, but always had it. Maybe it was the artist in him. Maybe it was that he lived with his aunt, not his parents. Maybe some kids like Maybeck understood stuff other kids didn't. He had this quality about him: part attitude, part confidence, part selfish.

"Have you seen the others?" Finn asked.

"Just got here," Maybeck answered.

Finn checked his front pocket for the Return, a

small device—like a garage door clicker or key fob. The Return shut down the DHI server and allowed the Keepers to wake up wherever they'd fallen asleep. Without the Return, the Keepers could get stuck as DHIs. Finn felt a sense of relief to find the device where it belonged.

The Kingdom Keepers seldom arrived at once. It depended upon when a person fell asleep. Maybeck and Finn sat next to each other on the low wall surrounding the statue. The night air was cool. Somewhere backstage trucks were groaning.

"Are you okay with this?" Finn asked.

"I understand wanting Amanda and Jess to be with us." Maybeck's voice tightened. "Finding Wayne will be easier with Jess. And I get that they come as a pair. But it's a hassle, and it's dangerous for Philby to try to turn them into DHIs. That's all."

"Understood," Finn said.

"We don't know what's real and what isn't. We don't understand what happens when we cross over. Most of the time I can't even believe we have. Holograms? Seriously?" Maybeck sounded so uncertain.

Finn found it unsettling. Maybeck was typically overconfident. Finn looked around, hoping someone else would arrive. The Park was creepy when it was empty and dark.

"We voted on it," Finn reminded him.

"I was in the minority. Imagine that."

"Why do you do that?" Finn asked.

"Do what?"

"You know exactly what I'm talking about."

"Point out that I'm different?" Maybeck asked. "Finn, I'm black. Deal with it. I am different. I'll always feel different. Not better. Not worse. Just different. Besides, it's me, Finn. It's like Philby and his brain, or Charlene being hot. I'm not saying that makes me special, just different. You're different, too. We're all different."

"Then why make a point of it?"

"I don't know. I'm African American. So what? Right? There's good parts of that and bad parts."

"I don't think of you as different. I don't even see that part of you anymore. Maybe I'm supposed to, maybe it's disrespectful. I don't mean it like that."

Maybeck eyed him. "But I'm cool, right? You see that, right?"

"Shut up," Finn said, smiling.

Philby crossed over. He arrived lying down on the pavement staring up at the sky.

"I don't think I'll ever get used to this." Philby sat up.

Maybeck spotted Charlene and Willa. "We're all here," he announced.

The others gathered around, all five kids standing

in front of the statue of Walt Disney. For a moment everything felt right. They'd been there before many times. Had been there together. Every one of them was smiling.

"Philby, do you really think our DHIs will work outside of the Magic Kingdom?" Willa asked.

"We've never done that before," Maybeck said, sounding concerned.

"There are DHI projectors in Hollywood Studios now," Philby said. "They project *us* there as guides. It makes sense that we should be able to see ourselves, see each other, once we're there. When we're away from the projectors, I don't know, it's like when we're inside the teepee, I think. We're still there, but we're in DHI shadow so our holograms can't be seen. The point is, we're still physically there. We can pick up stuff and we can be hurt, even if we can't be seen."

"By the Overtakers," said Charlene.

"Yeah, that's the point," Philby said. "We're still at risk."

The five DHIs glowed slightly. Static sparked off Philby's hologram. He slipped the paper into his pocket and the static lessened.

"Let's face it," Finn said, "there's a lot more that we don't understand than what we do."

Philby spoke quietly. "I would suggest we avoid all

contact with any people we may see. And no talking. If we get separated, we meet at the entrance of Pixar."

"Agreed," said Finn. The others nodded.

"Honestly, I'm a little scared," Willa said.

"We're all a little scared," Finn said.

"Speak for yourself," said Maybeck.

"Okay," Willa said, "let's get to it."

12

AMANDA SAT UP, knocking an assignment off her lap. Ms. Nash was calling for both her and Jess from downstairs.

Jess swung her legs off her lower bunk. Ms. Nash never called out from downstairs. She came to their room and summoned them. Scolded them. Bossed them around. Shouting at Nash House was strictly forbidden and universally punished.

Jess stood. Amanda slipped off her bunk to the floor. Jeannie didn't so much as look over.

Amanda wasn't sure how to respond.

"No way am I going to shout back to her," Amanda said.

"No, that wouldn't be smart," Jess said, agreeing. The girls finger-combed their hair (Ms. Nash was a stickler about appearances) and hurried out of the bedroom.

"Girls?" Ms. Nash sounded so . . . sweet.

"Maybe she's had a stroke," Jess said.

Amanda coughed up a nervous laugh.

Sneaking a peek downstairs, the girls saw a tall woman standing inside the front door. She looked old—at least thirty. Properly attired, hair perfectly coifed, it took Amanda a moment to realize who she was.

"It's her," Amanda gasped. She grabbed Jess by the arm.

"Who?" Jess asked.

"Her. I'm not wrong. She's the one who was watching the school. I'm guessing she's also the one who followed Finn."

"You're sure?"

"Pretty sure."

"Girls?" Some of the sweetness in Ms. Nash's voice had soured.

The girls descended the stairs hand in hand.

"You have a visitor," Ms. Nash said. "This is Ms. Alcott, from the Timmerand School in Charlottesville, Virginia." She introduced the girls to the woman using only their first names. She led the way into the living area with its small television.

Ms. Alcott spoke softly, yet forcefully. "If I could visit with the girls in private?"

Ms. Nash looked as if she'd been slapped in the face. "Of course," she said.

"The four of us can have a discussion just as soon as I've had a chance to visit with the girls."

"By all means," Ms. Nash said, clearly upset. She left, pulling the two doors shut behind her.

Ms. Alcott studied the girls carefully.

"Can I trust you?"

Neither girl answered.

"Why, you look terrified, child," she said to Amanda. "Am I scaring you? I promise you there's nothing to fear." She lowered her voice. "I'm not from Timmerand School, though I am on their board of trustees, and I did attend there, years ago. I find the telling of small lies is most convenient. I do not advocate the practice as it's an extremely delicate matter. Bending the truth is like pulling back a spring—more often than not it snaps back and hits you. Stings like the dickens when it does."

"Why have you been following my friend?" Amanda asked, careful not to mention Finn by name.

"For the same reason I've come here this evening," Ms. Alcott said. "Because I need your help. And, I believe you need mine as well."

"I don't understand." Amanda glanced quickly at Jess hoping for some support.

Jess said nothing, never taking her attention off their visitor.

"Wayne," Ms. Alcott said.

Amanda swallowed dryly. That was not what she'd expected the woman to say.

"What about him?" Amanda asked. She pleaded to

Jess with her eyes: *Say something!* But Jess remained the same: unflinching, barely breathing.

"Your friends are his only hope. The Kingdom Keepers," Ms. Alcott said. "Finn Whitman, Terry Maybeck."

"We know our friends," Jess said, her voice ghostly. "You have something of Wayne's. What is it?"

Ms. Alcott inhaled sharply and leaned back into her chair. "Now how on earth could you possibly know that?"

"What is it you have?" Jess said. "What is so important?"

"I need to get it to Finn. I suppose one of the others might do, but Finn would be the best. I've tried several times to make contact, but it hasn't worked out."

"You stalked him," Amanda said.

"I'm an adult. You all are minors. That makes things difficult sometimes. Furthermore, I had to make sure the Overtakers were not following me or him."

Mention of the Overtakers by his woman gave Amanda a chill. "Are you saying there are Overtakers outside the Parks?" Amanda said. "Is that possible?"

"Wayne has always believed so. But he tends toward the paranoid when it comes to his enemies. I have no proof either way. But he warned me of it. I've always taken his warnings seriously."

"You've known Wayne a long time," Amanda said.

"You might say that," she said with a wry smile. "You see, I'm his daughter. Wanda Alcott, not Kresky. Wanda. Get it? Like Mickey's wand?"

"Aha," Amanda said, her thoughts spinning.

"What is it?" Jess said, repeating herself. "What have you brought for Finn?"

"My father has an active imagination. It's why he was such a successful Imagineer. He's also a bit of a kook, as I'm sure you and your friends have realized. The polite way to put it is to say he's eccentric. That's my father: eccentric. He claims he can 'see' things. You know, not with his eyes, but his imagination. Little things mostly. He'll mention someone's name and minutes later that very person calls him on the phone. Or he'll predict things. The power going out. A car running a stop sign. It's uncanny, really. As a child I considered them coincidences. But as I grew older, I had to wonder. I came to think of him as prescient. That means—"

"We know," Amanda said. "Your knowing something before it happens." She sneaked a look at Jess. "It's a gift."

"Or a curse," said Jess, winking at Amanda. "You still haven't told us what he gave you," Jess added.

"I didn't say he gave it to me," Wanda said, correcting her. "I told you I have to get something to Finn."

"Or the others," Amanda said.

"Just so."

"Before we agree to help you, I'd like to see what it is," Jess said.

"Of course." Wanda reached into her purse. "He made this the day before all that craziness at Animal Kingdom, the day before he disappeared. He'd kept everything about your friends private until then. I hadn't heard anything about it. But we spoke that day. He told me about the Overtakers, about Finn and Maybeck and the others. I'm wondering now if he called me because he foresaw his being captured. I think he may have been laying the groundwork for your friends to rescue him."

Wanda withdrew an item from her purse. She opened her palm, revealing a small, white cube. It was made of typing paper. There were symbols written and drawn on the cube's six surfaces.

Jess picked it up and studied it. She spun it, examining the various images.

"We can get it to Finn," Jess said, not wanting to surrender it.

"Thank you! As soon as possible, please!"

"Tomorrow," Amanda said. "I'll see Finn tomorrow."

"I can help you and your friends," Wanda said. "Until we get my dad back. I want to help."

"We'll give it to Finn, but Philby will be the one with the answers," Jess said. "He's smart. He might know what it means."

"I looked up each symbol on the Internet," Wanda said. "They were all easy enough to find. But none of it added up. And who can tell what order they're supposed to be in? Without the order, the message—if there even is a message—keeps changing."

"We'll pass it along," Amanda said.

"I do want to help," the woman said. "Access to the Parks. Research materials. I'm very close to my father. I know a good deal about the Overtakers, Maleficent, even Chernabog. I'm not claiming to be as useful as my father—there's only one Wayne. But I want to help."

"We'll tell them," Amanda said.

"I want to leave you with my phone number," Wanda said, scribbling out a number and offering it first toward Jess, but then passing it to Amanda, as Jess's concentration remained fixed on the paper cube she held. "Day or night. Doesn't matter. Please call."

"Okay."

"Thank you, girls. I will take care of Ms. Nash," Wanda said. "I'll say we're recruiting you as boarding students. I'll have the school mail some brochures. I can make it convincing."

"Your small lies," said Amanda.

"You do pay attention! I realize it's asking a lot to expect you to trust me." Her voice choked. "My father has spent most of his life making the Parks magical places. He invented the DHI technology. The Overtakers will do whatever is necessary to corrupt the Parks, to drive guests away. I'm not going to allow everything my father has worked for to be taken away. Not without a fight. My father believes in your friends. I've never doubted my father, never will."

"What's it like?" Jess asked, her voice soft and comforting.

"Excuse me?" Wanda asked.

"Having a father?" Jess said. "Neither of us knew our fathers." Her voice trailed off.

"Oh, I'm so sorry, dear. That's deeply unfair."

Amanda swallowed. She had a decision to make that wasn't easy. "Our friends are taking a risk tonight. If you are serious about helping them, I think they could use it."

Wanda pursed her lips. Her eyes welled with tears. "Thank you! Thank you so much for trusting me! You won't be sorry," she said. "I promise."

13

For the Kingdom Keepers, traveling from the Magic Kingdom to Hollywood Studios was a journey. Their DHIs stopped projecting, giving them an eerie sense of what it was like to be invisible. Things Finn took for granted, like having a bus driver hold the door open, didn't happen. That meant only he, Charlene, and Philby made it onto the first bus. Willa and Maybeck were left behind.

Until he and the others reached Disney Hollywood Studios, he'd had no idea who had made it and who had not.

Approaching the entrance, the three of them materialized. They waited, and finally Maybeck and Willa appeared out of thin air.

Finn spotted two night watchmen in time to warn his team. They hid until the guards disappeared into the Park.

They waited a few minutes to be safe, and then headed into the Park. "Willa, you're with Philby and Maybeck. Charlene and I will team up. We'll meet inside Soundstage B in ten minutes."

"What's the exact mission?" Charlene asked Finn.

"To scout the soundstage and figure out a way to shoot video of Amanda and Jess so Philby can process them as DHIs. Before we try to bring those two into the Park, we have to have a plan."

"The Overtakers have planted insiders in every Park. We know that's true."

"So, we'd better hurry," Finn said.

Soundstage B came into view. A cream-colored building, it loomed large from backstage.

"Someone's coming," Charlene warned.

Finn looked back and saw a woman.

"Dang!" he said.

She seemed in a hurry to reach them.

"What now?" Charlene asked.

"We're busted. If we run it'll be bad. I think we should act out our roles as Park guides. Like there's a glitch. We recite the same lines as our DHIs."

"I hope you're kidding. My memory isn't so great."

The woman closed the distance.

"Wait a second!" Finn said in a hushed voice. "That's the woman who followed me at school!"

"So what do we do?" Charlene asked.

"Look, you take off," Finn said. "Get to the sound-stage and wait for the others. If I don't show up, don't sweat it. Just get what Philby needs." He passed her the Return fob that could cancel their projections.

"This is no time to get all heroic there, pal." Charlene sounded concerned. "No way we're leaving without you, Finn."

"You'd better!" he said.

The woman reached Finn. They stood a few yards apart.

"You're Finn," she said.

"I know who I am. Who are you?"

"Amanda told me I would probably find you here."

"That's a lie."

"It's not. Do you want to call her?" She offered him her phone.

Finn stepped forward and waved his arm through her and the phone.

She gasped.

"Just so we're all clear about things," Finn said.

"I've heard the technology described so many times. But . . . in person . . . it's really quite amazing."

"What do you want?" he said.

"Amanda said you might need some help."

"I'm fine, thank you."

"It's not you," she said. "It's about Wayne."

"What do you know about Wayne?"

"That he's gone missing," she said. "That you and your friends are the key to finding him."

"I think you should go now."

"I'm Wayne's daughter, Wanda Alcott."

"What?"

"He said you're a natural leader. Said that you're the smartest one of the group."

"Then he lied." Finn swallowed dryly. "That would be Phil— That would be one of my friends."

"Philby," she said.

He felt a chill. Only Overtakers knew so much.

Charlene was now out of sight. He'd bought her enough time.

Wanda's smile reminded Finn of Wayne. It made him uncomfortable.

"You're going to have to decide if you trust me or not."

"Not."

"Your first time in the Magic Kingdom as a hologram, your very first time, you were near the flagpole. My dad was there. He told you to look at the moon because he knew that would help you later when you got back home." Finn felt as if somehow all the oxygen had been sucked from the air. He thought he might faint.

"I can help you, Finn. I can guess what you're doing. It won't be easy getting Amanda and Jess into the Park. Have you thought about that? I can help! And you and your friends can help me find my father. Please." Wanda reached into her purse. "I gave this to Jessica earlier tonight. She was going to give it to you, but we decided first I would try to find you here tonight. Time is of the essence. She and Amanda said Philby should see it."

"I don't believe you," he said, but it was a lie. He did believe her—he just didn't want to.

Her hand came out of the purse. Resting in her palm was a small white paper box.

14

WHEN WANDA ALCOTT PRODUCED a sizable set of keys from her purse and unlocked the door to Soundstage B, Finn began to believe her.

It wasn't exactly obvious. She had auburn hair, a pleasant face, and vivid green eyes. She was wearing loose brown pants, a scoop-neck top, and a black sweater. Her earrings were silver cursive letter Ds, the first letter of the trademark Disney logo.

Despite everything, Finn didn't fully trust her. After offering him the paper box she had asked for it back and had placed it into her purse.

"I'll go first," Finn said.

He consulted the others inside Soundstage B. "It could be a trap." Finn eyed the woman though the soundstage's open door. Wanda merely smiled at him.

"She does look like him," said Maybeck.

Wanda called to them. "Jessica isn't the only one who has vivid dreams. My father has the same ability. I think he knew trouble was coming. Jessica and Amanda told me you'd be here tonight, and that's why I've come. You do whatever you have to do in there. I'll stand guard out here. If you hear me bump against the door, you'll know there's trouble. Open the back door and leave it open, making it look like you left the building. But hide inside instead. Once they take the bait, I can help you leave the Park."

"Okay," Finn said. He shut the door, leaving Wanda outside.

Finn and the Keepers stood inside the familiar windowless, cavernous structure. They had each modeled here—their movements and voices digitized into talking holograms. Sometimes they'd work with a director alone. Sometimes in groups. A football field would have easily fit inside. Maybeck found some switches and turned on a row of lights. The lights hung from high overhead. The entire back wall was painted a vivid green.

It was here that Finn recalled weeks spent dressed in stretchy green suits wearing motion sensors. Seeing the place brought back all sorts of fun memories.

"We're not the same as when we first came here," Maybeck said.

"Kind of weird, you know?" Finn said.

"Yeah."

They searched the interior, including the two bathrooms, a small office, changing rooms, and a control room filled with electronics.

Maybeck climbed a ladder well up into the catwalks and rigging above the soundstage. His voice echoed as he called out, "There's no one here. We're good."

Philby barked directions. "Give me a few minutes. Willa, see if there are green suits Amanda and Jess can use. Maybeck, you and Charlene see if you can figure out the ropes and pulleys. No sense in doing this if we can't project them in action."

"There's just one problem," Willa said, "and it's a big one. Amanda and Jessica are grounded. There's no way to get them here."

Finn told them about Wanda's offer to help get the girls into the Park. He didn't like the idea of involving Wanda and he told them so.

Willa shot Finn a cautionary look.

"What?" Finn asked.

"It's just that, they've been put onto the Disney Park Security watch list. They won't be allowed in because they jumped the Living with the Land ride. If Wanda can help us with that, shouldn't we ask her to?"

Finn stepped outside to speak with the woman. It felt almost as if she'd been expecting him. He didn't like that, either.

"Yes, I can help with all of that," said Wanda. "Ms. Nash thinks I'm offering the girls a scholarship at a boarding school. I can get them away from her for a day or two by saying I'm taking them for a tour of the school."

Finn's face brightened. "That's good!"

"As for getting them into the Park: My father's a Disney Legend. I have connections."

The woman had claimed she'd come to help, and now Finn understood. He nodded, thinking of several things he could say, questions he could ask, doubts he could express. But the woman was offering to help, and they needed all the help they could get.

"When?" Willa asked.

"How soon can you do this?" Finn asked.

"Name a time. I'll have the girls here."

"Can you get us in here as well, not as DHIs but as our real selves?"

"I believe I can, yes."

"Then it's agreed," Finn said. "We'll set up a time. We'll meet here. Philby will work his magic and build holograms for both of them."

"And then we'll rescue Wayne," Wanda said. "That's the deal."

"Yeah, that's the deal."

15

WANDA ALCOTT'S PLAN WORKED. At 10:00 p.m. Friday night, she and the two "sisters" met up with Keepers backstage at Disney's Hollywood Studios. They all waited patiently as Philby prepared the computers in the control room of Soundstage B. Again, Wanda kept watch out front.

Finn and Philby had told their parents that they'd been invited to a sleepover at Maybeck's. (Maybeck's Aunt Jelly had agreed to go along with telling the white lie because Maybeck told her it was life-or-death.) Wanda had informed Ms. Nash that she was taking Amanda and Jess on a weekend tour of the boarding school in Virginia. In fact, the girls would be staying at Wanda's condominium Friday and Saturday nights. Philby was going to try to create their holograms in two nights—a process that could normally take several weeks.

Jess and Amanda changed into skintight green motion capture suits—leotards and tights, booties, gloves, and full hoods that covered their faces.

White dots peppered the motion capture suits. The dots helped the computers measure movement.

The girls took turns on the green stage. Philby directed them to squat, stand, walk, lie down, run, crawl, dance, and jump. He asked for dozens of combinations of movements as an array of sixteen video cameras captured it all. As Philby began asking for voice recordings, Wanda called out a warning that Finn heard in his ear buds.

"Red flag!"

Without hesitation, Finn repeated the warning into the cavernous soundstage. The Keepers had prepared for such a possibility. Willa stood ready to kill the overhead lights. Philby put the control room computers into sleep mode. Finn and Charlene shut down the stand-alone lights and all the cameras. Jess and Amanda worked to disconnect the cables from their harnesses.

The kids scattered to their predetermined hiding places.

Jess struggled. "Mandy, help me!" Her harness wouldn't unclip.

Finn, who'd hidden behind a wall of plywood panels, watched helplessly as Amanda tried to disconnect the harness.

"Go!" Jess said to Amanda. But Amanda kept trying to help. Jess swatted her hands away. "Hide! Now!"

Amanda ran. Jess fell flat onto the stage. The green of her suit and harness, even the green cables, blended perfectly into the green backdrop, the green canvas floor, and the green wall behind. She vanished.

The lights went dark. The soundstage door swung open.

The lights switched on.

"See? What'd I tell you? Nothing! So what's all the fuss about?"

A second voice spoke, echoing in the vast room. "The report was that Pollock heard something as he drove by in a golf cart, not that he saw something. Maybe something was left on. We ought to look around."

Footsteps crossed the soundstage. A moment later the two men appeared in the only crack of a view that Finn had.

Peering out he saw Jess facedown with the two uniformed guards heading directly toward her.

One of the guards lit up a cigarette.

"You can't smoke in here," his partner said.

"Correction: I can't smoke out there. No one's going to see me smoking in here, unless, I suppose, you're going to turn me in?"

"No."

"Then what's the problem?"

"No problem."

"Okay, then."

The smoker remained where he was. The other guard grew restless and headed in the direction of the control room. Philby was hiding somewhere inside—and the room was not very big. "You know what they used this place for?" the smoker called out. "I mean, other than the movies? Those hologram kids."

"DHIs," the other called back.

"Yeah, that."

"I wouldn't mind being a hologram. Then I could stay home and watch the game while my hologram walked the Park all night."

"Careful," said the smoker, "or maybe we'll be out of our jobs someday."

"Security Guards Two-Point-Oh," said the other guy, laughing.

He entered the control room. Finn lost sight of him. Poor Jess was only a few yards from the smoker.

The man took another drag off his cigarette. He exhaled in Jess's direction.

Don't cough! Finn willed.

The smoker got restless and started walking.

Finn spotted a group of push pins stuck into the plywood. He pulled one out of the wood and threw it across the soundstage as a distraction. It clattered and rolled.

The smoker turned away from Jess.

"Hey!" the smoker called out.

The other guard reappeared. Maybe Finn had just saved Philby as well. "What?"

"Heard something . . . I don't know . . . over there."

"So check it out, you doofus. And put out that ciga-rette before you burn down the place."

The smoker smudged out the burning cigarette against the sole of his shoe and headed in the direction of the push pin. The other guy said, "This is a nonevent." He used a radio that hissed when he turned it on. "This is Nester and Johnson. All clear on Soundstage B."

The two men made for the door.

Finn had to keep himself from laughing. "All clear on Soundstage B." *All-clear* was exactly what Philby was trying to create for the girls.

Five minutes passed. One by one the kids stepped out from their hiding places. Finn helped Jess to her feet.

"We've got to keep it down. Not so loud," Philby said. "We still need to get a bunch done before we fin-ish up."

"Not tonight," Finn said. "That was too close. And besides, look at the time."

They were a half hour behind schedule.

"Those guys aren't coming back tonight. Let's get busy. We can be done here in two hours if we hurry."

"I think I sweated through my suit," Jess said, checking her armpits.

"You did great," Finn said a little too adoringly. Amanda stared down Finn. Charlene saw it all.

16

WELL BEFORE MIDNIGHT ON SUNDAY, the five Kingdom Keepers had all gone to bed in order to cross over as holograms into the Magic Kingdom. After two long nights of work in the soundstage, Philby had as much data as he needed to create "minimal DHIs" for Amanda and Jess.

From the Magic Kingdom, the plan was to split up. Charlene, Maybeck, and Willa would keep watch. Philby and Finn had a mission to accomplish.

While the other Keepers were assigned various backstage exits, Finn and Philby had to reach the Park servers located in a secure room in Magic Kingdom's Utilidor tunnels. Philby needed to load Amanda's and Jess's profiles onto the DHI mainframe in order for the two girls to cross over. Once into the tunnels, the two boys passed a few Cast Members and maintenance crew. All the Keepers had dressed in their DHI costumes. Finn and Philby played their parts as DHIs. They waved or nodded to others in the tunnels and tried to look as if they belonged. All the time they felt like imposters and were certain they were going to be busted.

Philby, who managed to keep a million facts in his head at once, led Finn through the maze of interconnecting tunnels.

"Our DHIs will pass through the locked door, no problem," Philby said. "But if there are people inside the server room, we are going to have to have an excuse for why we're in there."

"After closing hours on a Sunday night?" Finn said. "You really think there will be anyone in there?"

"Well, if there are, and if they see us and decide to shut down the server, we're in big trouble. Dangerous trouble." Philby spoke in a voice filled with worry—not a typical state for him. "All of us would be trapped in the Syndrome until the servers are switched back on tomorrow morning. We'll be lying in our beds at home like we're zombies."

"We're either doing this, or we're not," Finn said. "It's a little late to cancel. Think of Wayne. Think of Jess's dream. Wayne's in trouble and we're pretty sure he's in Epcot, and he needs us. End of story."

Philby looked over at Finn and nodded. "You're right."

Philby stopped in front of an unmarked door. "This is us."

A pair of voices came from the far end of the tunnel. They had to hurry.

Together, the boys stepped through the door. Finn turned around and made sure the door was still locked. Nothing had changed. It was all good.

"Heaven!" said Philby, spreading his arms as he faced the stacks of servers.

Philby searched row after row of servers, inspecting the labels taped beneath each black brick. He located a vertical column of six blinking boxes as well as a keyboard and screen beneath them. Within a few minutes, he was working the DHI data.

He typed frantically.

"Done a little bit of this, have you?" Finn asked.

"For me," Philby said, never slowing, "this is like a violinist playing a Stratosphere—"

"Stradivarius," Finn corrected him.

"Whatever. Just like that. I love messing with this stuff. First, I'll move the girl's imaging to the mainframe. Then I'll grant permission for their imaging to be projected in all the Parks, just like us. And if I can figure out the code, I'm going to grant myself access to this baby so I can control what Park we land in when we cross over after going to sleep. That'll save us from landing here in the Magic Kingdom and having to get ourselves to Epcot or wherever."

"Can you lift the DHI curfew?" Finn reminded.

"Already done."

"So are we out of here?"

"Patience. It's going to take me a couple more minutes, and then I'm going to check the server for any unusual cold spots in Epcot."

"Maleficent," Finn said. She spread cold the way a pig spreads smells.

"Exactly. If we know where she's been, maybe we find Wayne."

17

FOR THE NEXT DAY AND A HALF the texts flew back and forth between the Kingdom Keepers. At school lunches Finn told Amanda what was happening. Philby had continued to work on Amanda's and Jess's DHI data. Charlene was consumed with trying out for a dancing part in a school pageant.

"What about Maybeck?" Amanda asked as Finn ate what was supposed to be mashed potatoes.

"He texted that Philby should bring him the paper box this afternoon, after school. Maybeck said he figured something out."

"That sounds promising," Amanda said.

"What about Jess?" Finn asked.

"She's fine," Amanda answered dismissively, without a moment's thought.

"I'm just asking," he said.

"Who said you weren't?"

"As in: Has she had any more . . . uh-oh."

Lousy Luowski was headed in their direction. He carried a tray with only a dish of jiggling lime green Jell-O. Finn thought he had a pretty good idea what Luowski had in mind for the Jell-O.

"Hello, Greg," Amanda said in a disarmingly kind voice.

Her pleasant tone stopped Luowski in his tracks. The dish of Jell-O bumped against the lip of his tray and stopped.

"We've got some unfinished business," Luowski told Finn. Mike Horton nodded at his side, like a translator.

"Greg," Amanda said softly, drawing him in. "Have you heard about the wind here at school?"

"That's a trick question," Mike Horton spoke into Luowski's ear. "Wind is invisible, in the first place."

"That's a trick question," Luowski said to Amanda.

"Think hard, Mike," she said. "Science class about a month ago when Denny Fenner shoved Lois Long into the corner."

"And all the beakers went flying off." Horton stopped himself from laughing.

"And broke all over the floor," Amanda said.

Horton nodded, his skin going pale.

"What's going on?" Luowski asked, taking another determined step toward Finn.

"It wasn't pretty," Horton answered.

Luowski took the dish of Jell-O in hand. He held it over the top of Finn's head.

"What I've heard," Amanda said, her attention fixed

on Luowski, "is that the wind is actually like some kind of ghost that inhabits the school. It defends the innocent."

At that moment, Luowski's hair lifted off his oily face, blowing straight back. His shirtsleeves fluttered and rippled. Horton's hair was caught by the wind as well, but not nearly in the same way. Luowski had to lean forward steeply just in order to remain standing.

"What . . . the . . . bleep . . . is . . . happening?" The terror in the boy's eyes made Amanda smirk. If he stood up straight, he was going to be blown over backward. More important, the green Jell-O cubes were no longer square. They were stretched into weird shapes and moving. Several of them skidded across the dish. One by one they lifted out of the dish, splattering onto Luowski's shirt.

"Stop it!" Luowski shouted at Finn.

Finn shrugged.

"Stop it, you witch!" Luowski said to Amanda.

"Me?" she gasped, backing her chair up as if afraid of it. "I don't think ghosts listen to bullies, Greg. I've heard you have to scream to get their attention. You have to scream an apology."

The wind doubled in strength.

Luowski now leaned forward like a ski jumper just to remain standing.

Other students turned to see what was going on. Amanda continued to stare at Luowski. The boy's face was pale with fear.

"I don't think they can hear you," Amanda said.

"I'm sorry! I'm *so-o-o-o-o* sorry!" Luowski crowed like a rooster.

At that exact instant, the Jell-O flew off the dish and into Luowski's face. For a moment he wore a slimy green mask with only his eyeballs visible.

The wind stopped at once. It was like a door slamming shut. The forward-leaning Luowski fell flat on his face. Most of the kids in the cafeteria cheered.

Finn looked across the table to see Amanda's face. She wore a wide smile. She chortled, covered her laugh, and looked away from Luowski. She and Finn met eyes. Finn shook his head faintly. Although amused, he didn't approve of her making an enemy out of Luowski.

"I think the school ghost likes you, Greg," Amanda said. She picked up her tray and stood. "I'd be careful not to threaten other students from now on."

The green-faced Luowski rolled over and looked up at Finn. He started to speak but stopped himself. Instead, he turned and growled at Mike Horton, who couldn't stop laughing.

Finn caught up to Amanda. "You shouldn't have done that."

"Where are we meeting after school?" Amanda asked him. They stood at the trash cans dumping what should have been mashed potatoes off their plates.

"I didn't know you could *push* like that. Without your hands," Finn mumbled.

"There are all sorts of things I can do that you don't know about, Finn."

"You can't just . . . do that in school."

"Of course I can," she said. "Who's going to believe anyone can do something like that? There will be a dozen explanations for what happened to Greg. None will involve me. Just wait and see."

They left the cafeteria heading for their lockers.

"Do other Fairlies act so—"

"Bravely?" she said, interrupting.

"I was thinking more like . . . stupidly," he said.

"Ha-ha!"

"I'm serious. That was stupid."

"Greg Luowski was going to smear green Jell-O into your hair. The least you could do is thank me."

"You're right. Thank you. But you should follow the same rules as the rest of us. You're a DHI now. You can't draw suspicion."

"I'm a DHI who's about to be sent back to Maryland to a halfway house full of Fairlies. I'm desperate, Finn."

"And how is misbehaving going to help your situation?"

"How's it going to hurt it?" she asked. "If I can do a little good before I leave, isn't that better than doing nothing at all?"

He knew he should have an answer for that. Even something trite would have been welcome. But a part of him understood that she was right. When it came to doing good, it was better to do something risky than to do nothing at all. He felt the same way about attempting to find Wayne.

"Where and when are you meeting?" she asked. Finn was heading one direction, Amanda the other.

"Jelly's store after school. We're making plans for tonight. You and Jess are part of it."

"We're crossing over?" Amanda said excitedly. "It'll be our first time."

"You're crossing over."

"Gotcha," she said.

As she walked away it almost looked like a stiff wind was blowing at her back.

18

THE KEEPERS WAITED twenty minutes for Jess and Amanda's DHIs to arrive outside of Epcot. When they did, Philby received a good number of pats on the back for his work. Willa hugged him, causing both embarrassment. The sisters moved carefully and played tricks, like swiping their arms through solid objects. Each of the five Keepers could remember testing his or her hologram's "invisibility." Seeing the girls doing the same, hearing their giggles, made each of them marvel in the magic of being a hologram.

Having studied the location of the Epcot security cameras, Philby took the lead. He kept the group to the sides of the Park where he could and sent them running quickly across open spaces. With their holograms capable of walking through walls, Philby moved them into and through buildings wherever possible. Jess and Amanda thrilled at their new ability, especially when projection failed inside some buildings and the group literally went invisible.

"You know," Amanda said at one point, "if I'd known how much fun this is, I wouldn't have felt so sorry for you all."

Within a short time their DHIs were climbing a staircase that led to the VIP lounge in the Seas with Nemo and Friends pavilion.

The lounge's dark wood paneling, retro furniture, wall decorations, and acrylic piano were a throwback to 1980s decor. A large metal sculpture of a fish stared out from one wall. But the prize of the room was the window into Nemo's five-million-gallon aquarium. It offered dazzling views and endless visual thrills as fish and sea animals swam past.

"Kelp," Finn said, pointing from the center of the room. The group had spread out. They all turned as Finn spoke.

"Did you say, 'Help'?" Amanda asked.

"Just like in Jess's drawing," said Finn, still pointing. "The seaweed. And that chair. That's where Wayne sat."

Everyone looked at Jess. She felt the eyes on her. "Yes. You're right, Finn. That's what I saw. That's what I drew."

"And that's why you're here," Charlene said. "To confirm that for us."

"Does it mean anything more to you?" Amanda asked Jess. "Is it speaking to you?"

"Art is that way for me," Maybeck said. "I draw something, and it comes alive in my head."

"I can see his breath." Jess sounded timid, perhaps

afraid of being laughed at. "I know that sounds stupid but—"

"Nothing sounds stupid to us," Philby said. "Seven holograms standing in a room where someone dreamed the future. If we spoke that aloud they'd lock us up in the funny farm. Get real. None of this is possible, and yet it's impossible to deny."

"Breath," Finn repeated. "I wonder what that's about?"

"It's certainly not cold in here," Charlene said. "Not cold enough to see your breath."

"Wayne doesn't smoke," Maybeck said, "or vape."

"So disgusting," Willa muttered.

"Breath," Charlene said.

"Breath," said Willa.

"I've got it!" Philby said. "Everybody over here." He moved to the aquarium's glass wall. When the others hesitated, he barked the same instruction at them.

They moved as a group.

"Spread out in a line."

"Who put you in charge?" Maybeck asked.

"Let's do it." Finn understood when to play the leader, and when to allow others to lead. Wayne had taught him this. He looked at the empty chair, wishing Wayne were still sitting there.

The seven kids spread out in a line facing the glass.

"What now?" Willa asked.

"We all take one step closer. We breathe onto the glass. We fog it. You know? Like when you're bored in the backseat of a car."

"You're kidding, right?" Maybeck laughed a forced laugh like everyone was supposed to laugh with him, but no one did. Instead, they all started blowing onto the glass.

"Handprint," Charlene said.

"Nose and mouth," said Willa.

"Aww. Someone drew a heart around a fish. How cute is that?"

"We're not looking for cute, Amanda." Philby used his Professor Philby voice. They all took him seriously when he did that. "Everyone move a little bit lower. We don't want to miss anything."

"I'm getting dizzy," Maybeck said.

"No joke," said Finn.

"I think this is Mickey Mouse in a scuba tank," Jess said. "But it's not a very good drawing."

"Another heart."

"Two fish kissing," said Willa.

"Hang on!" Philby's professor voice declared. "I think I've got it. And I'm right behind that chair, so it makes even more sense." Instinctively, the others gathered behind Philby. He waited for them. He turned his head to make sure they could all see. But there was something more to his expression. A warning? Was he scared?

Philby leaned forward and blew against the glass. He revealed a perfectly drawn three-dimensional cube. In the forward square was drawn a *W*.

"He drew a monogrammed ice cube?" Willa said, clearly meaning it as a joke. No one laughed.

"No," Maybeck said, perhaps voicing what some of the others were already thinking. "That's the paper box Wanda gave Finn. The paper box he left for us."

Finn had taken apart the paper box so it would lie flat and fit into his pocket. Handing it to Maybeck he was met with scorn for having "wrecked it." But it wasn't wrecked, and Maybeck had it folded as a cube in no time. He passed it to Willa, who passed it on to Charlene. No one seemed to want it. Philby accepted it from Charlene. He spun it in his fingers, studying the odd markings.

"I just don't get it," Philby said.

"That's the first time I've heard you say that," Willa said. She didn't sound disappointed, more like worried.

"You know how Wayne leaves us clues? Tricky clues. Things we can solve that the Overtakers maybe can't." Philby looked hopefully at Willa.

"Yeah?" she said.

"We're missing something. This cube is one of those. It's like that. It's all here, but it's not. We're supposed to figure it out."

"Figure out what?" Charlene asked. "What's he trying to tell us? Why is he always so opaque?"

Maybeck's face twisted. He mumbled to himself. He might have said, "Opaque?" Or maybe it was, "Cake?" or even "Quake?" There was something about his expression, something about his not being his typically loud self that won the attention of the others. They waited for him to say something. Not so much out of courtesy, but more curiosity.

With everyone watching, Maybeck returned to the aquarium's glass wall. He blew on the glass, fogging it in the same place Philby had. The finger drawing of a cube reappeared. "Not opaque, Charlene, but transparent. The only way fogging glass works is when there's light behind it."

"Technically, it's translucent."

"Shut up, Philby, I'm having a brainstorm," Maybeck said.

"Oh, pardon me." Philby's feelings could be hurt way too easily. He backed away from Maybeck.

"Wayne's giving us two clues. First, pay attention to the paper box. Second, that it's . . . translucent," he said, nodding to Philby. "Show them."

For the briefest of moments Philby seemed not to understand. Then, looking at the paper box in the palm of his hand, he told Willa it was too dark in the lounge. He needed a bright light. Currently the Keepers didn't carry cell phones in their pockets when crossing over. Something about the process caused the batteries to overheat hot enough to burn. Philby was working on fixing that.

Charlene called out for help. She and Finn stacked one chair on top of another. Charlene the gymnast climbed up like she was part of a street fair show. She licked her fingers and touched a spotlight, aiming it away from the aquarium and directly at Philby. Finn helped her down.

Delicately pinching the box between his thumb and index finger, Philby lifted the box into the beam of bright light. He laughed quietly, knowingly, as he spun the box. By then, Maybeck was stooping to match Philby's perspective.

"What is it?" Willa asked.

"It's translucent. Transparent. Just as Maybeck said."

"The shapes line up." Maybeck's voice thrilled. "Front side of the cube with the back square."

"Forming letters," Philby said.

"Forming letters," Maybeck said. "N."

Philby rotated the box. "O." And again. "P."

"That's it," Philby said after a few more rotations. "P, O, N."

"An abbreviation?" Willa proposed. "A code? We all know how much Wayne loves codes. A word scramble?"

"Piano," Amanda said. "An N, a P, and an O."

"Again. More," Philby encouraged. "As few extra letters as possible." The group started calling out words. "Nope." "Pond." "National Painters Organization." "Natural Organic Plants." "Overtakers Patriot Nation!" The group went quiet. The mention of the Overtakers disturbed them all.

"O-P-N. Open," Jess said. "He's telling you to open the box."

"I opened it before," Finn said. "There's nothing written on the inside. Besides, if there was, Maybeck and Philby would have seen it in the light."

"Jess is right. That is so Wayne," Willa said.

Maybeck carefully found the edge that tucked into the box and used his fingernail to pry it up. The box came undone. Maybeck opened it, avoiding where Finn had creased it to fit it into his pocket.

"I've done this same thing in math a hundred times," said Philby. "It forms a—"

"Cross," said Maybeck. He lifted the shape to show the others. At the bottom of the four vertical panels that formed the stem of the cross was the small pointed piece used to tuck in and hold the box together.

"More like a yard sign." Charlene won a laugh. "The pointy part goes into the grass."

"Hang on!" said Finn, stepping closer to the unfolded box. "You're right! That's a point. A tip. But it's not a yard sign."

Philby nodded. "It's the tip of a sword."

Maybeck said a string of bad words.

"Only boys would see that as a sword," said Charlene cynically. "It's clearly a cross. A church? A cemetery? A chapel? A sign?"

"It's a sword," Philby the Professor stated. He didn't want any discussion about it.

"We don't know that." Charlene wasn't afraid of Philby. "This is Wayne, don't forget."

"Okay, people," Willa said. "It's either a cross, a yard sign, or a sword. We're in Epcot. The box drawn onto the glass is in Epcot. So, what matters is if we know of any crosses, yard signs, or swords in Epcot."

"And what any of those might mean," said Jess. "To us. To Wayne. Who knows?"

"China isn't Christian," Maybeck said. "So probably no crosses.

"Same with Morocco. We can rule out those areas in World Showcase."

"That is so ridiculous," Willa said. "There are millions of Christians in China, and probably Morocco, too. I did a history report on Egypt. Christians there, too. We have to consider all the countries, all the rides. There could be crosses or swords anywhere."

"We'll divide into teams," Philby said.

19

WILLA SAID WHAT CHARLENE and Jess were both thinking. "Notice there's no boy with us."

"I was sure they would require that," Charlene said. "They always think they're so brave and protective!"

"No kidding."

"You're stronger than any of them, Charlene." Amanda laughed at her own comment. "I'd love to see you arm wrestle Philby."

"He climbs rock walls," Charlene said. "I'd rather try Finn."

They giggled.

"No matter what, we can't be caught or get in trouble. The boys would never let us forget it!"

Walking around as dimly glowing holograms put everyone at risk. Willa moved them along connecting paths, next to walls and through buildings, seeking out DHI shadow—the locations where the hologram projection was weak or nonexistent.

The girls searched the Canada Pavilion for a sword or cross to no success. They hid behind the pavilion's music stage as a golf cart whizzed past heading back toward the Park entrance.

"Do you think the characters come out at night in Epcot like they do in Magic Kingdom?" Amanda asked.

"I'm sure they do," Charlene said.

"Epcot has a lot going on after hours," Willa said. "With all the plants, all the food—"

"I love the food here!" Charlene said.

"So, if the characters do come out, it's probably much later."

"I'd just as soon not be around for that," Jess said. "I don't need to see the Tomb Warriors or Sadness tonight. Just let's find Wayne and get out of here."

"Hey, it was your dream that got us here."

"I know that. This is one time I'd love to be wrong."

"If we want to speed this up, we could each take a pavilion." Willa's practicality occasionally rubbed others the wrong way.

"As in alone?" Amanda said.

"Or pairs. Whatever."

"Willa, you and Amanda take France," said Charlene. "Jess and I will take England. You're right, it'll be much faster. Swords or crosses. Maybe a sign shaped like a cross."

They made plans to meet up under the entrance awning at Chefs de France.

20

CHARLENE TOOK JESS'S HAND. Crouching low, the two holograms flashed and shone as they cut through shadows on their way to England.

Willa waited with Amanda feeling something wasn't right. Amanda asked if they should get going. But Willa waited, looking carefully in both directions.

"Do you hear that?"

"Something cracking?" Amanda said.

"Wood?"

"Or ice, maybe."

Amanda glanced back over her shoulder. "Wood. Definitely wood."

The Canada Pavilion's tall totem at the top of the stairs was splitting apart. It consisted of four huge primitive heads stacked one atop the other. Each was the size of a clothes washer. The highest head had a pair of wings or arms, making it look the most human of the four. Major cracks appeared, separating one head from the next. As the one with wings broke free and lost its balance, the entire totem pole—all thirty feet of it—tipped forward.

Amanda and Willa stood in place, their shock preventing them from moving.

"We're holograms, right?" Amanda asked.

"I don't think we should trust that." She tugged a frozen Amanda out of the way as the totem collapsed and fell forward. Two of the heads rolled down the stairs like giant boulders. Or bowling balls—with Amanda and Willa more like bowling pins. The two heads bounced, crushing the concrete path. They both punched holes in the wall and fell into the lagoon, bobbing like apples in a Halloween dunking tub.

"Hurry!" Willa shouted. Above them, the top head, the one with the wings, was flying. *FLYING!* Its hooked beak and beady eyes aimed down at them.

Just as Amanda hit her stride, Willa punched her in the arm and knocked her over. The flying totem head dove so low its beak scratched the path, leaving a line of turquoise paint behind. Its mouth snapped shut, sounding like a door slamming.

"It's trying to eat us," Willa called out.

"Yeah? Well, I'm nobody's snack," Amanda shouted. She stood.

"Get down!"

Amanda remained standing, defiantly facing the flying object.

The flying head arced over the lagoon, its stubby

little wooden wings flapping. Turning, it aimed for the girls once again.

"Mandy! Down!" Willa cried out.

But Amanda stood her ground, her back straight, a look of pure determination on her face. The flying head straightened its wings and dove.

"Mandy!" Willa tried again, but to no avail. "To your left!"

The last of the heads marched toward Amanda in a waddle, rocking on its circular base, tilting side to side. A slow but steady approach, the mouth opened and closed, snapping loudly.

Amanda lifted her arms. Her palms opened.

Willa called out to her. "It won't work! You're a hologram."

Amanda drew her open palms to her shoulders and threw her hands forward in a unified *push*. Willa saw the air in front of the girl turn murky, like oil in water. It swirled and stirred and rolled in a mass toward the diving totem head. One of the totem's wings nearly tore loose as the wall of wind blasted the flying head. The thing tilted, its one good wing flapping frantically to keep it aloft. Amanda's roiling air churned like boiling water. The wind knocked the head out of the air. She turned, arms extended, moving the disturbed air with her. It was as if she had a magnet holding the head in her grasp. She delivered the flying head into the ugly snapping stump rocking its way toward the girls. There was the sound of a loud smack. The two heads rolled like bowling balls, bounced off a low wall, across the walkway, and back toward the stairs they had tumbled down.

Willa found Amanda in a trance, still staring up into the night sky. She reached for the girl's forearm, but her hologram swept through Amanda's. Focusing, Willa tried again, lightly taking hold. Holograms were tricky. "It's okay. We're good. You did it." Amanda seemed not to hear. Willa pulled gently. Amanda snapped out of it.

"France," Willa said. "Swords and crosses."

"Flying totems in Canada," Amanda whispered.

"You get used to it," Willa said encouragingly. "Sort of. Not really. And it's never the same. The Overtakers are getting better about cleaning up their mistakes. My guess? By tomorrow that totem will be standing right where it was."

"I don't like it," Amanda said.

"That's why we're here, Mandy. To stop it. That's what got Wayne in trouble in the first place. Overtakers. The more power they gain, the more danger for all of us. For all of Disney."

"France," Amanda said.

"Yes. France. One thing at a time."

21

CLIMBING THE STEPS of the Mexico Pavilion's ancient pyramid, Finn prepared himself for the emptiness and darkness he knew was about to greet him. Arriving through the doors, he walked past a sculpture and down some other stairs on his way to the marketplace in Plaza de los Amigos. The size of several basketball courts, the marketplace occupied the center of the pyramid. Dozens of shelves and tables, racks and stands displayed gifts and clothing. The marketplace was crafted to look like an outside plaza. Lantern-lit balconies looked out over the plaza while a blue-black night sky glowed from the far end of the room.

Finn looked around for any crosses or swords. He didn't love being inside the pavilion alone, but with Maybeck and Philby teaming up, he'd been the odd man out. He had more control over his hologram than any of the others. Even a small amount of fear could make his friends briefly "solid," meaning they could feel pain, or be injured. Finn's ability to go all-clear, overcoming such fear, made him less likely to be a victim. But all-clear didn't last long—only a minute or two—and it wasn't a switch he threw. He had to make himself calm down to bring it on, and that wasn't always the easiest thing to do.

In fact, being alone in the marketplace gave him the creeps. Being alone in any Park attraction after closing hours gave him the creeps. Being a hologram was supposed to make him safer. It didn't feel that way.

He searched a rack of necklaces, wondering if he might find a cross. Nothing. He rounded the rack and studied the artwork on T-shirts and sweatshirts. No crosses. No swords.

His arms tingled as the sound of castanets clicked and clacked. Dancers used the clapping instruments to create rhythms to songs. But there was no song playing, only the finger drumming, like sticks being banged together. He spun a full circle looking for the dancers.

"Hello?" he called out bravely. It sounded to him like they must be dancing inside a store on the opposite side of the plaza called La Tienda Encantada. He'd expected to be alone. He'd wanted to be alone. Dancers? Why now, after hours? The obvious answer for any Kingdom Keeper was: Overtakers. Far too often the Disney villains appeared after hours to disrupt the DHI efforts to follow clues or find ways to end the Overtakers. But dancers? Seriously? Were they going to try to make Finn dance with them? he wondered. It didn't strike him as the most dangerous threat.

Using the shelves and stands to hide behind, Finn moved quickly toward the store. He had to see what was going on. There was no way he was going to be able to focus with all that noise. He hid behind a bunch of baskets holding blankets for sale.

Peering around the baskets, he felt the very fear he was supposed to have control over. It wasn't dancers, and it wasn't castanets he was hearing.

He couldn't believe what he was seeing.

22

"You SEE THEM?" Charlene asked. "In the lights?"

"I do," Jess answered. "Two crosses. Each on top of a chimney. Should we tell the others?"

"Not until we check it out."

"But I thought—"

"No. We're not going to waste time. Wayne needs us. We need to keep going."

The crosses were perched atop a pair of chimneys on the building nearest to them. The two-story stone building in the England pavilion had been built on the other side of a small park. Inside the park was a monument on a pedestal. The girls tucked down low against the park bushes. Jess's heart beat hard and fast. The crosses seemed an obvious clue connecting the paper box to a possible hiding place where Wayne was being held by Overtakers. She and Charlene would save him.

"What now?" Jess asked.

"I can climb the wall up to the roof," Charlene said. "But it might be smarter to check the inside of the building first."

"I like that idea better."

"Our holograms can walk through the walls as long as we're calm. Are you calm, Jess?"

"Not exactly."

"Look, if anything freaks us in there, we can use the doors. But it's better not to trigger alarms, so going through the wall is always better. Deep breath, okay? If you're scared, you'll probably just bounce off the wall. That will leave me alone inside and you alone out here. That's not good."

"No, it's not. I get it." Jess took deep breaths. She pinched her eyes shut and focused deeply as she did when trying to find one of her daydreams. She felt her heart slow down, felt the stress lessen. She nodded. "Okay, I'm good."

"You'll go first, Jess, so I'm here as backup if you need me."

Jess thanked her. There was a tug of friendship between them, something Jess had experienced only with Amanda for a very long time.

Charlene led the way. Jess marveled at Charlene's confidence. Her determination. Nearing the wall, Charlene slowed allowing Jess to walk past. At the last moment, Jess closed her eyes. She exhaled. When she opened her eyes she was inside a store.

Charlene followed in behind her. "See? Just like we did earlier."

"Except then I didn't feel scared."

"You did great. Your first time being a DHI. It took me a bunch of times before I could do things like that. You're killing it, Jess!"

The store was called the Sportsman's Shoppe. It sold English soccer balls and sports jerseys. Decorated with silver award cups and trophies, it also held stuffed animals, toys, and T-shirts.

"Look!" Charlene pointed to the cash register desk.

"Yeah?"

"Up there."

"Oh, my!" Jess exclaimed. "How did I miss that?"

A knight's body armor stood on a small balcony above the main doors. The knight held some kind of spear. But on the wall hung an ugly-looking ax weapon that looked an awful lot like a sword.

"I think we're getting warm," Jess said. "Take a look over the fireplace."

Mounted above the large fireplace, behind a rack of sports jerseys, five ancient weapons fanned out on top of a red shield.

"Good one," Charlene said. Her voice was husky. She sounded excited.

"Crosses!" Jess pointed to the carved woodwork on a wooden peak above a glassed-in display. Beyond it, more weapons hung mounted to the wall.

"Charlie." The nickname slipped out of Jess without her thinking. "We really should tell the others. This has to be where Wayne meant with that paper box. I mean … come on! Crosses *and* swords."

"Weapons, yes. Swords? I haven't seen any."

The girls continued moving around the shop. They both stopped at the exact same moment. In front of them, a display offered a statuette of a knight on a horse. It was a beautiful piece of art, and the tag at its base said it was for sale. But it wasn't that piece that held the girls' attention. Behind the statuette hung a sword. A real sword. A big sword.

"How about now, Charlene? What about now? Isn't it time?" Jess was breathless. "Time to tell the others?"

First, a single clock tolled its bells. Twelve, midnight. It sounded quaint and charming.

"That's Big Ben, I'll bet," said Charlene. "I went to London with my mom in fifth grade. I heard it ring noon. It was so cool."

Another clock joined the first.

"Wow!" Jess said.

"Hang on," said Charlene. "It isn't midnight. It's eleven-forty-seven. The clocks shouldn't be—"

"Time." Jess raised her voice to be heard above the clocks. Another had started, and another. Four or five now, and each louder than the last. "I spoke that word. That's when it started. It's a—"

"Curse." Charlene pointed around the shop. In looking for swords and crosses she hadn't noticed how many of the items on sale included clocks. Small ones painted onto toys. Others on the walls.

Ten or twenty now, all ringing at once. They weren't stopping at twelve, and they weren't getting any quieter. Both girls had to shout to be heard.

"What's going on?" Jess called to Charlene.

"I don't like it."

"We should get out of here!"

Charlene pressed her hands over her ears. "My head is going to explode."

Jess ran for the exit. She hit the doors. Her hologram bounced off and struck the floor hard. She covered her ears just as Charlene had. "Locked!"

Thirty, forty clocks now. It was louder than a rock concert.

"Charlie! We're trapped in here."

Charlene sat frozen on the floor, her hands pressed to her ears. Something red oozed between her fingers.

23

ON HANDS AND KNEES to avoid being seen, Willa led Amanda from England over the footbridge and into France. She motioned for Amanda to stop. They squatted down behind a lighted cylinder of art posters from another country, another time. The miniature Eiffel Tower perched high at the back of the France pavilion shimmered with tiny white lights.

Willa pointed out a golf cart security patrol over by Italy. Amanda nodded. No matter what, they were not to be seen.

"There's another." Amanda pointed across the lagoon toward Spaceship Earth where another golf cart was moving counterclockwise around the lagoon.

"You doing okay?" Willa asked.

"I'm tired. When I *push* like I did with the heads it kind of beats me up."

"Now we know there are Overtakers in the Park tonight," Willa said.

"I wish we could signal the others." Amanda sounded vexed. "The really creepy part, Willa, is how you talk about the Overtakers so calmly."

"Yeah. You kind of get used to it."

"Not me, not ever." Amanda swiped her hologram hand through the concrete base supporting the cylinder. "Never."

"There may be things like perfume and soap in the stores," Willa said, "but I don't think we'll find swords."

"If the Hunchback was part of France, we'd find a cross for sure. But there's no church. So, where do we look?"

"Ratatouille," Willa answered. "What's a sword but a big knife?"

"Ooo! Good point! No pun intended."

The girls shared a laugh. Willa's eyes became serious. "Can I be honest about something?"

Amanda swallowed dryly as she nodded. She thought she knew what was coming—a thing between girls. It was called a boy. Amanda knew which boy. She just didn't know what to say.

"Since Charlene auditioned to be a DHI, she has liked Finn. I mean not just as a friend."

"I know what you mean."

"I know you like him, too. I think everybody likes Finn."

"He's not my boyfriend," Amanda said. "I don't have a boyfriend. I don't want a boyfriend. Charlene is gorgeous. She's a cheerleader, a gymnast. It's not like I stand a chance against someone like her."

"Give me a break, Amanda. We've all seen the way he looks at you. The way he blushes because he cares what you think about him. We all have. I have. I just wanted to say that some of it bothered Charlene at first. She doesn't lose at much. She wanted to be mad at you. She was mad at you. At him. But she's never going to tell you any of this. I'm pretty sure she's over it. That's all I wanted to tell you. She's not mad at you or anything."

"Jess says boys are like the weather: they change for no reason when you least expect it. I like Finn. I do. But Jess and I are a team. We escaped the 'school' in Baltimore—it was more like a prison—and all we care about is not being caught and sent back there. I don't have time for boys. Charlene can do whatever she wants. I'm focused on survival. That's a little more important than boyfriends. Jess and I are determined to get our friends out of that horrible fake school in Baltimore."

Willa reached out and touched Amanda's hand. "Maybe we all can help you two with that."

"Maybe so." Amanda changed in that instant. Willa could feel she was keeping something from her. She could see it in her face. A secret. Not a boy secret. Not a Finn Whitman secret. Something that lived deeper inside Amanda, something that mattered.

"Okay, they turned around. Let's go. Me first. Keep up with me. Ready?"

Amanda dipped her chin, nodding slightly.

Willa walked—fast!—but in a crooked line. It took Amanda a moment to realize the girl was trying to move in and out of shadows. Their holograms stood out the most in dark shadows or bright lights. In the murky world of gray the girls dimmed slightly.

Amanda was led through the entrance to the Ratatouille ride. Willa hunched low, looking back to make sure Amanda was as well. They reached the loading dock where separate vehicles could take on passengers and follow different tracks. Willa jumped down off the loading dock, since the ride was shut down after hours. Amanda followed her.

"It's dark in here," Amanda said.

"All the attractions use emergency lights at night. We've been in so many of them, I should know. If we're lucky, we just walk through, see nothing, and get out of here."

"Because the option is?"

"We've told you all the stories. You saw what went down in the Animal Kingdom. And the heads in Canada just now!"

"Everything is so gigantic. I don't like it." They were

surrounded by bottles forty feet high. Vegetables. Pots and pans. A dead fish.

"We're the rats," Charlene said.

"Yeah, I get it. I don't want to be a rat."

"I don't think we have a choice."

The girls walked side by side. They'd entered a different world. The emergency lighting etched strange shadows on the walls, ceiling, and floor. A giant corncob cast a slanting black shape that looked like an eggplant. Chimney tops towered up ahead. A fish the size of a building.

Willa jumped several feet to the side so fast Amanda only saw her land. Before Amanda could ask what was going on, Willa explained herself. "That's Skinner up ahead."

"The Chef."

"Yeah."

"And?"

"I saw his arm move. Just a twitch. But it moved! Skinner doesn't like rats. He hits them with rolling pins. He sets traps."

"And we're the rats."

"Now you're paying attention."

"He's a giant," Amanda said, seeing only the chef's elbow. "He's like Gulliver!"

"More like King Kong, but yeah."

"So let's turn around."

"How can we?" Willa sounded super stressed. "Of all the characters in here, who's going to have a knife?"

"A chef. Yeah, I get it."

"And if he does have a knife. A man his size, a knife that size—"

"Is more like a sword to us. Right. So we can't turn around. Wonderful."

"I'm afraid not. We may need your talents to separate him from a knife, if he has one."

"You want me to push the knife out of his hand," Amanda said.

"Or from his costume. Or the set. Yes. Can you do that?"

"I can try, I suppose."

"Good. Then, here we go. Try not to be afraid. It makes you more human than hologram. Being human hurts. Really hurts."

"Willa, if you did see him move, if he really did move, then does that mean what I think it means?"

"If the ride is alive, if the characters have come alive, it means we need to move fast and think slow. Nothing you expect to happen happens. Things you've never even thought of happen."

"That's reassuring."

"I try."

They moved cautiously, one delicate step at a time. Willa crossed them to the opposite wall so that they might sneak up on Chef Skinner. They hadn't moved but a few feet when the floor began to shake.

An old lady's growling voice called from behind them. No amount of French accent could make it sound pleasant. "I can smell you, you pesky vermin! You do not dare to poke out the little wet, black noses or I will, of course, fill them with the little rock salts. Me, and my double-barrel smoothbore. Same as I keep those *chiens* out of the rubbish."

"Smell us?" Amanda whispered. "That's just not right."

"Here's how this is going to go down," Willa said, pressing her back to the wall and pulling Amanda beside her. "That'll be Mabel, probably as tall as a crane. She hates rats, meaning you and me. The barrel of her shotgun will be as wide and round as a Giant Sequoia tree. We need to stay away from her. She doesn't just talk about shooting. She pulls the trigger."

Amanda swallowed dryly, unable to get a word out.

"I'm no Charlene, but I do climb climbing walls. I'm going up this wall to look for any knives the Chef may have." She pointed to a massive shadow approaching the corner behind them. That shadow was Mabel. That shadow was Mabel's shotgun. That shadow was trouble.

"Tired or not, you're going to have to stop her, Amanda. Her and Skinner, especially if I manage to steal his knife. Chefs love their knives the way musicians love their instruments. The way a kid loves a puppy. Get it? Chef is not going to like me taking his cutlery. You understand?"

"I can't push twice in a row like that. I mean, not right away I can't. For one thing I'm a hologram, or half-hologram. For another, it doesn't work that way. Not when I'm this tired."

"You're going to have to try. We're out of options!"

24

Philby whispered to Maybeck, "I don't like this statue warrior guy. He reminds me of what happened at Small World."

"I hear you," returned Maybeck in an equally soft voice. "If he came after us, that would be bad news."

Inside the entrance plaza of the Norway Pavilion, a large statue of a Viking warrior stood valiantly holding a long sword. The bearded, armored warrior seemed to be looking right at Philby. "But that's a sword in his hand."

"That's definitely a sword. But it's plaster."

"Hopefully, it stays right where it is. And if it's plaster that doesn't help us. It can't be Wayne's message." Philby looked deeper into the Norway courtyard. "Frozen Ever After isn't going to turn up a cross or a sword. We could try the gift shop, I suppose."

"What about this place?" Maybeck indicated the Stave Church, a small wood building with tall, sharply angled roofs.

"I haven't been inside since they made it into the Viking museum."

"Well, this dude's a Viking and he's carrying," said Maybeck.

"So, we should check it out."

The boys walked around the statue, both keeping some distance. Arriving at the church's front door, Maybeck gestured for Philby to go first. "Chicken," Philby said. He was only teasing, but Maybeck took it the wrong way. His hologram jumped in front of Philby's and vanished through the door.

Philby followed. The room was small, with displays on every wall. An enormous tree trunk filled the center of the tight space. Elaborate carvings had been cut from it. A goddess faced them. She had a peaceful face and long curls of hair cascading over her shoulders. Maybeck pointed out her sword. Philby told him her name was Freya, a Norse mythological god of war and the afterlife. "If she were real, she wouldn't be afraid to use that sword," he said. "She and Odin accept dead warriors into different versions of heaven. Hers is a beautiful green meadow."

"Pass," Maybeck said. "No desire to die tonight."

They circled the carved tree trunk. Philby called out the names of the Nordic gods. "Loki's the one with the knife. Odin the spear—"

"Thor. I'd like to have that hammer!"

"You wouldn't be able to lift it."

"I've seen the movies, Philby. Give me a break."

"There!" Philby headed quickly to Odin's display. box. A framed painting hung on the wall. A brass animal horn curved at the bottom of the case. But it was the iron sword, rust colored, dented by a blacksmith's hammer that held their attention.

Maybeck reached for it.

Philby tried to stop him. "Don't disturb it!"

But Maybeck wasn't one for superstition. He took hold. The sword didn't budge. It had been secured to the wall in several places and wasn't going anywhere.

Philby said, "A cross, and we're inside a church. A sword on full display. Can it get any closer to Wayne's paper box? This has got to be it. Wayne's somewhere in Norway. We need to tell the others."

"Dude! Frieda." Maybeck's finger aimed at the carved tree trunk.

"Freya!" Philby corrected.

"Frieda, Freya, I don't care what you call her. That lady's eyes just moved."

25

WILLA CLIMBED THE RATATOUILLE wall carefully. Chef's elbow stuck out, now about five feet away.

"I smell zee rats!" called Mabel, in her thick French accent.

"Not in my kitchen you don't." Chef's thunderous voice caused the wall to rattle.

Having little to grip, instead of using handholds Willa squeezed herself into a crack between pieces of scenery. She spread her legs and arms out against a giant carrot and a smaller bell pepper. Inch by inch she lessened the pressure on an arm or a leg and moved higher. It was a delicate mix of strength and balance. Over ten feet up the wall, if she fell now it wouldn't be pretty.

Mabel turned the corner. She carried a massive shotgun in both hands. Willa looked down onto the top of Amanda's head. The girl had pressed herself into a shadow directly below. Months earlier, when this same kind of thing had happened in Small World, Willa had been terrified. What couldn't possibly ever happen— the dolls coming alive—had happened. She worried about Amanda, assuming she had to be scared. Facing a twenty-five-foot-tall character from a favorite movie could get one's heart beating quickly.

Chef's arm was six feet thick. It was made of some kind of white plastic. Slippery, Willa thought. Dangerous. Rather than try to climb it, she decided to move around and stand on top of the arm if possible. It turned out to be a good decision.

Chef's elbow flexed. The rest of him appeared as he moved in the direction of Mabel. There was big, and then there was bigger. Chef was bigger. Willa drew a deep breath. She exhaled slowly trying to calm herself. By moving his arm, Chef left a cavity in the wall. It was like a skate park half-pipe. Willa pulled herself up and into it. Her body hurt. Between her nerves and exertion, she struggled for air. She pulled herself along the half-pipe, moving toward Chef. Looking down toward his waist she saw only the chef's white jacket. No sash. No knife. One of the waist pockets bulged with something big. A giant onion, or potato perhaps.

Disappointed, she kept moving, wanting a look past where Chef had been standing. Maybe there would be a kitchen counter there. Maybe there would be a knife—a sword. Or maybe she'd see Wayne tied up in a bowl of vegetables and this would all be over.

"There have been disturbances," Chef said.

130

"I have heard this," Mabel said.

"A problem in Canada."

"Oui."

"We must move him." Chef's enormous right arm swung down and covered the lumpy pocket on his jacket. "La Mère Verte would demand this of us."

"Oui."

"You will find a small vegetable crate, perhaps?" Chef wasn't asking; he was telling her.

"I could put it with zee others. This is good. Most excellent idea, Chef."

"You will see to it."

"As soon as I take care of zee rats."

"I told you: no rats in my kitchen."

Mabel sniffed. If Amanda and Willa hadn't been holograms, the wind might have knocked them over.

"It smells of zee electricity. That, and a whiff of zee perfume. A lotion, perhaps."

"You need your nose fixed."

"You need your kitchen cleaned."

"That's your job, not mine," Chef said.

"You talk like that and I'll file a complaint."

"Stop your prattle and find a small crate." Chef lowered his right arm. To Willa, it looked like a tree falling. For an instant—only an instant—the movement of the jacket gave Willa a look down into the pocket.

Not a potato. Not an onion. Not Wayne's white hair. Whatever, whoever, was inside Chef's pocket, it was a creature.

A creature with horns.

26

SKULLS! HUMAN SKULLS! No longer on the shelves, but on Mexico's marketplace floor. Not just a few, but dozens of skulls all snapping their bony jaws. They looked like they were eating. Or like they were hungry.

They stretched in long lines, many rows deep.

An army of snapping skulls, Finn thought. Just my luck. The skulls were part of Mexico's celebration of the Day of the Dead. A little like Halloween and New Year's rolled into one. The skulls were for sale and supposed to be plastic. They looked like real bone to Finn. Real skulls.

They were alive.

They were coming for him. With each snap of their jaws the skulls rattled and moved forward. Not far. Not fast. But slow and steady.

And hungry.

Finn decided it was time to leave. He'd had enough of Mexico. He spun around.

Five skeletons, all wearing black bow ties and top hats, stood less than ten feet away. They carried walking canes with metal animal heads on top of the canes. A duck. A dog. An eagle. Their skeleton heads moved back and forth as their dark hollow eyes appraised Finn. They looked like curious dogs.

"Hello," Finn said.

All five began snapping their jaws like they were trying to talk, trying to answer him. One of the skeletons took a tentative step forward. When the other four moved in lockstep, Finn identified the one who had moved first as the leader. That was the one to deal with.

Meanwhile, a quick glance over his shoulder confirmed the continuing slow advance of the snapping skulls.

The skeleton leader raised his cane like a weapon. His squad did the same.

"Why would you want to hurt me?" Finn spoke aloud.

The jaws of all five skeletons frantically clapped teeth to bone.

"I don't speak Skeleton," Finn said, eyes dancing to locate something to use as a weapon. "My guess is you are Overtakers. If you want to hurt me, you might be protecting something. Something like an older man with white hair and ice-blue eyes. A former Imagineer who once knew Walt Disney. Does that happen to ring a bell?"

More snapping. This time, louder.

His arms tingled. Finn feared he'd lost some of his hologram, that he was partially solid and therefore able to be hurt. He didn't want to be hurt. The five skeletons stepped forward, their canes lifted. The battalion of skulls clattered and clacked while on their steady approach.

"What does a skeleton fear, I wonder," Finn said aloud, in part to hear his own voice, to steady himself. "A casket, I'll bet. A rectangular six-foot hole dug into the ground."

The five didn't like this. They started swinging the canes. Finn ducked and dodged the attempted blows. He looked for a way out. To his right and left stacks of shelves were covered in toys and trinkets. Behind him, the army of skulls were eating their way through the bottom of a stand of shelves! Wood splinters flew through the air. Directly in front, the swinging canes swooshed as the skeletons tried to thump him on the head.

Finn saw nothing close by that could be used to defend himself. A cane struck him on the shoulder.

It hurt! His hologram was weak.

Movement out of the corner of his eyes. A row of plush donkeys had come alive on a shelf. The small stuffed animals kicked each other off the shelf and to the floor.

He had two choices: tiptoe his way through the rows of skulls and risk getting his toes bitten off, or get through a wall of five tall, extremely nasty skeletons.

"You're not being fair. I'm ridiculously outnumbered," Finn spoke aloud.

Again, a cane struck him, this time on the side of head. Finn went dizzy.

A moment of pure panic caused him to reach down and pick up a skull, his fingers in the eye sockets. He held the snapping skull in front of him and managed to cause it to bite one of the skeleton arms swinging at him. The skull didn't just bite. It locked its jaw onto the skeleton's forearm and didn't let go. The weight of the skull lowered the arm of the skeleton. Before the skeleton could switch the cane to the other hand, Finn turned and kicked out, catching the skeleton in the ribs. The skull never let go of the skeleton, but the skeleton let go of the cane.

Finn snatched the cane out of the air as the skeleton fell and shattered.

He grabbed hold and started dueling with the leader. Canes, barking and cracking. Small splinters of wood flying.

27

*D*ING DONG. *Ding Dong. Ding Dong!*

Charlene and Jess pressed their hands to their ears while looking for a way out. Something had exploded inside Charlene's left ear. A loud popping sound, and a little blood. The ticking of the clocks rose to a deafening clamor. They boomed like fireworks.

Jess lay on the floor, having smacked into a door. "My hologram isn't working!" she said.

"It's because you're scared," Charlene screamed. "We're both scared!"

"What do we do?"

"I've got an idea, but the others won't like it. If we trip the fire alarm, it must unlock all the doors. But that will bring Security and they'll know someone's in the Park."

Jess glanced around the room. She shouted, "Do you remember which clock started first?"

Charlene's eyes roamed the room. "Maybe. Why?"

"I read a lot."

"So?"

"I may be able to break the curse."

"You're a witch?" A horrified Charlene took a step back from Jess.

"No, no! I told you! I'm a reader. There are several ways to break a curse. Water is one. But that would mean your fire alarm idea, and that's no good." Jess didn't want to remind Charlene that her ear was bleeding. Her bloody hand looked disgusting. It had to hurt. "We need to get out of here."

"We need the sword!"

"We can come back for it," Jess said. "If we break the curse, we lose our fear. If we lose our fear—"

"We can walk out of here as holograms."

"So, which clock?" Jess's head hurt from the volume of the clocks. Her teeth rattled.

"How should I know? I can't hear myself think!"

"One of the clocks started it. That's the only way we're going to stop it." Jess felt the ground spin. The screaming in her head—ding dong, ding dong—was making her dizzy. Her vision blurred.

"Jess? Can you hear me?"

Jess read Willa's lips. She couldn't actually hear much of anything. She thought she might throw up. Her head went gooey. The room went black.

Then, there was nothing.

28

MAYBECK TOOK A STEP BACK. "I would say that's impossible, but I know better."

"We need Odin's sword. A god's sword. We need to take it from him."

"Looks like you can tell him that yourself." Not only was the goddess Freya tearing herself from the bonds of the wooden column, but Odin's sculpture as well. "And that makes four," Maybeck said. All four Norwegian gods had come free of the column. Maybeck glanced to his side, but Philby was gone. "Chicken!" Maybeck shouted.

But as he turned around, he saw Philby prying Odin's sword from the case on the wall. Not only was Philby not chicken, but he was preparing to fight.

Philby raised the sword with two hands. It was incredibly heavy for his hologram to lift. He swung it side to side.

"Careful, that's my nose," Maybeck said, ducking.

"Grab something."

As sculpture, the four gods had been carved from the waist up. Now it was a show of horror as their legs and feet peeled from the wood, and they stepped onto the floor. Thor with his hammer. Freya, Odin, and Loki all holding weapons.

Philby held the sword, blade before his face. "We mean no harm."

Odin—the god of gods—looked away, turning his attention to one of the glassed-in displays. Sharply, he looked back at Philby.

"They're Norwegian, dude, and seven hundred years old. They don't speak English."

"They're mythological, Maybeck. Fictional characters."

"Do they look mythological?"

They looked dangerous. Angry. As a group, they fanned out, occupying more of the small space. Once again, Odin stole a look at the same display case.

Maybeck followed Odin's sight line. What was so special about that case? In another case Maybeck spotted a giant fishhook. It was rusted but ended in a point. It would make a decent weapon. He moved toward the case.

"Where are you going?" Philby sounded scared.

"I'm right here." Maybeck was a showoff. Always. Every waking minute. Even staring down four angry Norse gods holding weapons, he couldn't stop himself. He waved his hologram arm, making sure to win their attention, and then dropped it through the glass and into the display. The seven-hundred-year-old gods seemed to understand the impossibility of what Maybeck had just done. There were four fishhooks in the case. Maybeck yanked his DHI arm out of the case. He broke the glass with his elbow and took hold of the largest hook.

Three of the gods jumped back. Not Odin. He moved for the display case he'd been staring down.

"The horn!" Philby said. "The drinking horn! He's going to blow into it and call for others!"

The display held a curved metal horn that looked like it belonged on an animal head. But if Odin used it to sound an alarm, to summon more Norwegian guards—like the warrior statue outside—Philby and Maybeck wouldn't stand a chance. Philby rushed toward Odin and swung his sword. Odin had no choice but to engage. Their swords struck, but the sound was all wrong. It wasn't metal-to-metal. Even as he fought back, Odin continued looking at the horn in the case.

Loki lunged at Maybeck, thrusting the spear tip at Maybeck's chest. Not trusting his hologram, Maybeck swung the hook, catching the spear. He raked the spear to the side and sank the fishhook into Loki's upper leg.

It stuck there. Maybeck couldn't get it out.

"Philby! They're wood! They aren't human!" Maybeck wrestled to get the large hook out of the wooden leg. But he'd swung hard and the tip was stuck.

Loki, who clearly did not feel any pain from the hook, looked down at Maybeck, who was on his knees trying to get the hook free. Loki shortened his grip on the spear.

Maybeck saw Freya about to drop her sword onto his back. Instead of pulling, Maybeck pushed the hook. It cracked and splintered Loki's leg. More importantly, the effort turned Loki so that as Freya's sword fell, it cut Loki's spear in half.

"Eww," Maybeck said, as his fishhook pulled free. The splintered crack in Loki's wooden leg oozed yellow-brown tree sap. It looked more like thick yellow blood. Maybeck nearly hurled.

Thor raised his hammer over Philby's head. Philby ignored Odin and swung defensively at Thor. A large chunk of wood flew from Thor's forearm. A repulsive blob of discolored sap splatted onto the floor.

Philby swung again. Another chunk of wood dislodged. More sap.

"Chop the weapons loose!" Philby called out.

Maybeck swung the hook. It stabbed into Freya's sword. A wooden, not metal, sword. He pulled. The sword cracked at the handle and fell to the floor, broken.

Philby slid on his knees and swung hard at Odin's nearest leg. Odin's clenched fist smashed through the glass case. Philby shielded his eyes while delivering a second and third blow just below Odin's knee. More of the icky sap seeped from the wound. Odin's fingers made a cracking sound as he reached for the horn. Philby swung again at the leg. And again. More wood chips—the gash in the leg deepened. A blob of sap dripped down the statue's leg.

A loud snapping sound.

Odin tilted as his lower leg fell away.

But the horn came to his lips as Odin fell.

Maybeck body-blocked Freya. She leaned off balance. Maybeck cracked her with her own wooden sword. The goddess fell backward. As she smashed to the floor, her long curls of hair broke off her head. Her eyes went wide. She reached back and grabbed her broken hair and swung it at Maybeck. He jumped high and landed on both her knees. Freya's legs cracked in half.

The drinking horn sounded. A note rang out like a high-pitched foghorn.

Philby's sword cut off Odin's chin. There would be no more horn blowing.

Thor's hammer clapped down onto Philby's partial hologram. It hurt something wicked. Philby fell face-first to the floor.

Maybeck hooked Thor's hammer and pulled Thor to the floor. He jumped onto Thor's arm. The hammer snapped loose.

"You all right?" Maybeck called, turning to deal with Loki.

The door burst open. It was the Norwegian warrior from the statue outside. He was nearly too tall and too wide to fit through the door. He squeezed through, breaking the door frame, and he raised his sword.

He was not made of wood.

29

CHERNABOG! WILLA WAS NO expert on all things Disney. But she didn't need Wikipedia to identify the evilest of all Disney demons. Chernabog was said to "eat human souls." That was enough for her.

What the demon was doing in Chef's pocket was anybody's guess. Chef's pocket had to be at least six feet high. Chernabog's horns now rose another foot higher. The thing looked up at Chef. It was a face of half-man, half-bull. It made ugly look cute. His arms were said to double as wings. Willa had no desire to find out if that were true.

The demon growled as Chef fingered open the jacket pocket. It wasn't the growl of a lion. Not the growl of a gorilla. It came from some dark and forbidden place. It sounded to Willa like the sound of death—whatever that was. It made her go cold. It made her frightened.

She wasn't the only one: Chef's face had gone the color of his jacket.

"You are safe here, Redeemer. We are following your orders. Your pilgrimage to the old land is arranged as planned. It is only a matter of hiding you a bit longer."

Mabel was upon the Chef. She spoke softly to the demon. "You find any rats in there"—she racked the shotgun—"you just let me know. Say zee word."

"Mabel! Do as we discussed."

"We didn't discuss. You ordered me."

"Get a crate and get it quickly. Trouble in the Park is trouble for us. Trouble for the Redeemer."

Chernabog released another earsplitting holler. Willa's stomach turned. No knives, she thought, reminding herself of why she'd climbed the wall. No swords. Only a giant Chef talking to a demonic monster, and an old biddy with an itchy trigger finger.

The demon coughed up another disgusting sound. Part burp, part rocks rolling down a hill.

"Understood, my liege." Chef lifted his eyes to the darkness overhead. His lips moved silently. He looked almost to be praying.

"Forget the crate for now," Chef told Mabel. "Find Maleficent, Ursula, the Judge. Whoever you can. And hurry. The intruders must be stopped. The Redeemer has spoken."

"I will send our friends," Mabel said.

The shadow Willa's hologram occupied began to feel sticky. It began to *feel*. How, she wondered, could she feel a shadow?

Her thought was answered. Every shadow in the

ride began to slither like a snake. Some were thin and two feet long; others, twelve feet and thick. They slithered off the walls onto the floor. Shadow snakes! They slithered toward Amanda.

30

WITH HIS FINGERS IN THE EYE sockets of the snapping skull, and his thumb in the nose hole, something felt familiar to Finn. He couldn't identify it at first. He had never held a human skull—even a plastic one! As he dueled the four remaining skeletons with the cane, it came to him: bowling!

BOWLING!

Behind him: several dozen snapping skulls steadily moving toward his ankles. In front of him: four freaky skeletons swinging canes.

BOWLING! Of course!

Finn bounded backward. Swiping the cane with his left hand, he carefully avoided the biting teeth of the nearest skull. He picked it up. Standing, he took aim. Wrist back. Arm straight, it moved like a pendulum. Release.

The first try went all wobbly. The skull missed. It tumbled between two of the oncoming skeletons. Finn dropped the cane and focused on his bowling technique. Another skull. He put more *umph* into it. He hit and broke the leg of a skeleton. It tried to walk on the missing leg and fell down, bones shattering.

The other skeletons watched their comrade fall. They looked up at Finn. Unsure how a faceless skeleton could look angry, Finn nonetheless saw vengeance. Skull by skull, he continued to bowl. He missed. He grazed. He hit! Another skeleton fell. Two to go.

More importantly, with only two skeletons remaining standing, they no longer blocked Finn's escape.

He threw a snapping skull at the nearest skeleton and took off running. He crunched through the shattered bones on his way to the exit. Epcot had come alive, just like Magic Kingdom and Animal Kingdom before it.

Overtakers!

He had to warn the others!

31

CHARLENE KNEW WHAT had to be done. With Jess lying on the floor, possibly unconscious, it was up to her to do it.

Remember! she told herself. Which clock had started the racket? She and Jess had been standing in a different area of the room. She'd heard the sound to her left. Or was it her right?

The thunderous ticking of the clocks didn't help her. It felt like she was being hit in the head by a hundred hammers. One ear couldn't hear at all.

She walked unsteadily as she moved. Finding a place that felt familiar, she stopped. Looked. Listened, with her one good ear. She recalled the tone of the first clock. A low, bell-like chime. Almost as if it had come from afar. The tolling that had followed had been different—cheaper sounding. Smaller.

Charlene looked around for a possible source of that first rich bell tone. She saw and heard some clock-face teapots on a shelf. The sound was too thin. So, where had that real bell tower sound come from?

Her bad ear ached. The jet engine volume of

the tolling clocks had her head spinning. If she stayed in the room much longer, she would end up on the floor like Jess.

In the room! That's it! she thought. The first bell had sounded far off. As in: Outside! Could she leave Jess? Did she have a choice?

The closer she came to the display holding the room's only full sword, the louder the bells. She had thought it couldn't possibly get any louder. She'd been wrong.

One hand pressed tightly against her good ear, Charlene reached the display and took hold of the sword. The weight of it felt majestic. Regal. Royal. She could see herself as a knight in full armor, a lady warrior at the round table of Sir Galahad. She looked for something smaller and grabbed a dagger as well. Never enough knives, she told herself. Overtakers always outnumbered the Keepers.

She drew the shining blade from the scabbard. The steel blinked. Maybe it was her hologram; maybe her fear. The sword felt so heavy.

She charged to the front door and lowered the blade. Sparks flew as the blade struck the metal of the door lock. The double doors broke open. Alarms sounded. She had to hurry! Outside now, the original bells could be heard more clearly. Charlene ran in that direction.

A tall tower held a clock face. It looked painted onto the tower, but there was no question that the sound of the bells came from behind it.

Charlene chose the dagger. Lighter. Smaller. She took aim high overhead and hurled the small knife. It smacked into the wall next to the clock and fell to the cobbled path below.

She retrieved the blade and threw it at the clock a second time. Missed. The dagger fell again.

Was it her imagination, or were the bells coming from the store suddenly louder? Were the clocks angry with her?

She held the dagger by the tip this time. She drew it back over her shoulder carefully. Her eye remained on the prize: the clock on the wall.

She planted her feet, took aim, and threw. The blade spun end over end, like a propeller. Charlene's eye remained exactly where it had been focused: on the clock.

The dagger stuck into the clock face, close to the clock's minute hand.

The bells had stopped. The alarm continued to sound.

Had she not been alone, she might have cheered.

Jess staggered out the doors of the Sportsman's Shoppe.

Charlene found herself facing the Crown and Crest. Something drew her to the shop. She felt the urgent need to check on Jess, but she would have to wait one minute. First, Charlene set down the sword and walked her hologram through and into the store.

There, in front of her she saw what they'd all been looking for: an entire case filled with swords. The sword hilts formed perfect crosses.

32

Philby and Maybeck took two steps back. Odin's using the horn to call reinforcements left the boys facing an epic giant of a Norse warrior. He had seemed big when posed outside as a statue. Inside, he was ginormous.

"You think we can talk to him about this?" Maybeck said.

"His sword is as big as I am," Philby sputtered.

"Sword!" Maybeck exclaimed.

As the warrior stepped forward, the entire Stave Church shook. The statue's knees, hips, and ankles were cracked.

"He does not look happy." Philby's voice quavered.

"Your sword! Philby, you're holding Odin's sword. What if that makes you powerful? More powerful than Giant Man?"

"I don't feel powerful."

"Switch!" Maybeck passed Philby Loki's wooden weapon. He took possession of Odin's ancient sword. Holding it with both hands, Maybeck lifted it. He carried it in front of himself as he took two dangerous steps toward the warrior.

"Kneel to the sword of Odin. Lord of the Norse. Soldier of the gods. Leader of all armies."

The statue stood still. His massive head cocked to one side, studying the outstretched sword.

"I said kneel and be knighted!" Maybeck commanded. He whispered to Philby, "What's this dude made of?"

"Plaster. I think he's plaster."

The giant warrior dropped to one knee. His shoulders straightened.

"Statue Man. Great warrior of the Norse. I hereby anoint you protector of the Stave Church, defender of the realm. By the power of Odin's sword do I challenge you to serve these two boys as you would the gods themselves."

"You're getting a little over your skis, Maybeck." Philby's hoarse voice revealed the terror he was trying to hide. "Take it down a notch! How about he just lets us go?"

Maybeck raised his voice, paying no attention to his friend. "You will serve these boys to your death." He stepped closer to the giant, his hologram heart pounding. He tapped the giant's shoulder with the flat surface of the blade. Raised and carried it over the giant's head. Tapped the opposite shoulder. "I do declare you Knight of the Realm, Protector of the Boys."

Maybeck stepped back.

For a moment—nothing. Philby, Maybeck and the giant stood absolutely still.

The giant bowed his head in subservience.

33

"SNAKES!" Amanda cried.

"Rats!" Mabel hollered. She fired the shotgun, blowing rock salt into a nearby wall but missing Amanda. Willa jumped. Her hologram fell onto a snake, crushing it. She was five steps behind Amanda, who was already running for the exit.

"Don't run in a straight line!" Willa called out. Snakes tangled at her feet. She tiptoed and danced through their slithering ugliness.

Amanda took to running in a zigzag pattern. The next shotgun blast barely missed.

Whack! The end of a huge rolling pin punched a hole in the floor of the Ratatouille ride. Snakes flew in the air. Amanda cried out in terror. The rolling pin came on the end of Chef's arm. It showered Willa in debris. Pieces of concrete whipped through Willa's hologram. They didn't hurt! She was all-clear again. It was the best news of all.

"Test your arm!" Willa called. "Your hologram!"

She watched as Amanda swiped a zucchini.

Amanda's hologram arm went through the oversized squash. "Whoa!" she exclaimed.

"On three, we both jump through the wall to our left."

She heard the shotgun engage. Mabel wasn't going to miss this time. Willa knew it.

"Three!" she shouted, having no time for a countdown.

Both girls took a flying leap into a stalk of celery.

An explosion erupted behind him. Mabel had fired the shotgun, blowing a hole in the wall.

Amanda and Willa breathed fresh air. Outside air! They grabbed hands and ran.

34

As FINN'S MOTHER SLEPT, her body twitched in a serious convulsion that rocked the bed. She sat bolt upright, throwing the covers off the bed. Her husband reached down, pulled the covers back up, and went back to snoring.

She remembered something Finn had said.

"Wayne's missing."

How could she have been so stupid? Without meaning to, Finn spoke in a kind of code. Finn adored the old Imagineer. But would he break house rules to do something about it? Being a Disney Park guide was a blessing to their family. He'd earned a full college scholarship by modeling for his hologram. The family had a lifetime pass to all Disney Parks. But the problems since then—the danger—had required parental action.

Finn was not allowed to "cross over," as he described the glitch in the hologram software.

She threw her legs over the edge of the bed, tugged at her nightgown to straighten it, and hurried out of her bedroom and down the hall. Late or not, she had every right to check on her son. The family policy was, no lying.

She opened the door to his room, moved to the bed, and hesitated a moment as she saw the covers pulled up. Her son's peaceful face showed in the glow of his various electronics. She saw him as an infant, a young child, now a young man. She was very proud of him.

She wondered how she could have doubted him. Where had her trust gone?

She turned and took two steps back toward the door. She was about to leave the room when a voice told her something was wrong.

She turned back. She scanned the floor.

As a mom, she'd been working with Finn for five years—more like ten!—for him to pick up his clothes off the floor after he dressed for bed. Yet every morning, there were yesterday's clothes in a pile. Most of the time his room looked as if a tornado had hit.

So where were his clothes from the day before? Where were his shoes?

Her worry, her concern for her child resurfaced. She marched to the bed and pulled back the covers.

Fully dressed. Including shoes.

She knew what was happening before she tried to shake him awake.

"Finn? Sweetheart?"

She shook him harder. "Finn!"

Not a twitch. Not a complaint. He didn't tell her to go away. He didn't move.

She stepped away from the bed, her bottom lip trembling. Tears formed. She shook him again.

Her tears fell onto his pillow.

"You did not do this. Tell me you did not do this! Come back! Please, come back!"

35

"**W**HO'S HE?" Willa pointed to the Norse warrior alongside Philby and Maybeck. The Keepers, Amanda and Jess stood together under the Congressional dome in the American Adventure pavilion.

"Sorta like a bodyguard," Maybeck said.

Each of the Keepers reported their feats of survival in the various pavilions. Philby raised a finger to ask for quiet. The group stared at him. He nervously tapped the tip of Odin's sword onto the tile floor.

"Finn found crosses, but no swords in Mexico. Amanda and Willa found Chernabog. That's like finding a terrorist. Maybeck and I got Odin's sword."

"And our friend here," Maybeck said, interrupting.

"And him," Philby said, looking up at the plaster warrior.

"But Charlene and Jess! First, they spot crosses on the chimneys. Swords in two different shops. And time—the ticking clocks—running out. Both crosses and swords. That can't be coincidence. That has to mean something."

"Wayne's being held in the England pavilion?" Willa said.

"Could be," Finn said.

"Everything points toward the England pavilion." Philby's intense focus left everyone staring at him. Genius at Work. "But it's not the pavilion itself. That's too obvious for Wayne."

"We can't know that for sure," Charlene said.

"Two crosses on the chimneys," Willa said. "Double crosses. Double-crossed. Overtakers. Lies. Secrets."

"Nice," Philby said. "Excellent!"

"Odin's sword gave us control over our friend here," Maybeck said. "We used the power of its myth."

Philby tapped the sword on the floor. "The sword is charmed. As our leader, Finn, it belongs to you." Philby passed the sword to Finn. It was heavy, even for Finn's hologram. Finn accepted it.

"I don't like being called the leader—"

"But you are," said Amanda.

"All the clocks," Philby said. "The importance of time. We're running out of time."

"As in: Our parents are going to kill us for crossing over," Finn said. Everyone laughed.

"Wayne needs us," Philby said.

"I know what it is," Willa said. "I know what Wayne is trying to tell us."

"So?" Philby's impatience verged on anger.

"In all of Walt Disney World, where do we ever see a sword?" she asked.

"Sword and the Stone, Magic Kingdom," Jess said.

"Good one."

"If light sabers count, then Hollywood Studios and Star Wars." Maybeck looked around at the others. "I take it that means they don't count?" No one answered, but he got the message.

"Raiders of the Lost Ark, but the attraction is gone now."

"Peter Pan," said Amanda.

"That's an interesting one. The story is set in England. The ride is in the Magic Kingdom, not Epcot." Willa allowed her comment to marinate. "That's a connection almost as good as the England pavilion."

"Peter Pan's a dark ride," Maybeck said, trying to salvage his reputation. "Wayne could be hidden in the dark."

"That goes high on the list," said Philby.

"What else is there?" Charlene asked.

The Norse warrior moved for the first time in minutes. He stepped back, winning everyone's attention. Holding his sword in one hand, he awkwardly put his huge fists alongside the top of this head.

"Ears?" Maybeck said.

"Or Princess Leia's hair," said Amanda.

The warrior took his sword in both hands. The Keepers jumped back. The warrior reached the sword out and swiped dramatically. Intentionally slowly. He then returned to his soldierlike pose.

"Mickey," Jess said. "I drew Mickey in my journal. The ears he did with his fists. They're Mickey ears."

"Mickey. A sword? I don't think so," Maybeck said.

"Fantasmic!" Philby's eyes flared. His voice rose. "Mickey defeats the dragon in Fantasmic! He uses a sword or a flame."

"He uses his powers of thought," Willa said, correcting Philby—a rarity. "Maleficent becomes the dragon! She transforms into the dragon!" Willa said. "The Overtakers. Mickey does swing a thing that looks like a light saber."

"In *Fantasia*, the movie," Amanda said, "there's only music. No talking. The composer was an English conductor, originally from Poland." She got odd looks. "I like classical music. His name was Stokowski."

"We're in the wrong Park," Philby said. "Wayne led us here to find Odin's sword, to figure all this out. But he wants us in Fantasmic! And that's Hollywood Studios."

"It's past midnight," Jess said. "So, technically the next show is tonight."

"Time's running out," Philby said. "We all go to Fantasmic! tomorrow afternoon, before the night show!"

36

FINN WOKE UP IN HIS OWN BED. Moments earlier he had pushed the Return fob, sending his friends back to their beds as well. It was going to be a long day waiting to cross over into Hollywood Studios.

A check of the clock. He had time to change into pajamas and get a few hours of sleep.

When his alarm sounded a few short hours later, the house was far too quiet. His mother banged around the kitchen in the mornings as his father cooked. It was like she wanted to be noticed. Not today. Was she sick?

He showered and dressed. He left his clothes a mess on the floor. He grabbed his computer tablet and hurried down the stairs to the kitchen.

His mother sat at the end of the small table. A cup of coffee steamed by her left hand.

"Where's Dad?"

"Sit."

"Why isn't he cooking me—?"

"Sit. There's cereal. Eat the cereal."

Finn poured himself a bowl of Rice Chex and milk.

"I got him out of the house," his mother said. "I didn't want him hearing any of this. You can thank me later."

"Mom? Hear what?"

"Don't."

"What?"

"Don't act all innocent, Finn. It's unbecoming. It's dishonest."

Some cereal stuck in his throat. He pulled the bowl to his lips and washed down some sweet milk to dislodge it. He wiped away his milk mustache.

"We talked about this," she said. "We agreed."

"About?"

"I said, don't!"

"Okay! Okay! Sorry."

"How long have you been doing it? Breaking our agreement."

"It isn't just me. It's all of us."

"That makes it better? I don't think so."

"A couple times. That's all."

She exhaled. Lowered her eyes to the tabletop. She shook her head. "Remember what happened to Terry? When he didn't wake up?"

"SBS. Sleeping Beauty Syndrome. That's what we call it. It's when a hologram gets stuck and doesn't cross back over."

"He could have died. He could have stayed in a coma forever."

"Technically, I don't think that's true, Mom. Philby says—"

"Stop!"

Finn spilled some cereal off his spoon. He mopped it up with a paper napkin. "If we get caught. If our holograms are separated and one of us doesn't cross over, then yeah, our real self doesn't wake up. It looks like we're in a coma, but you know it's not that exactly. It's just that . . ." Her look told him to shut up. "Okay. I'm sorry, Mom."

"Wayne. It's about Mr. Kresky. You said he's missing."

"Did I?" That was stupid!

"No more crossing over. You understand me? You know what your father would do if he found out? He'd send you to live with your grandparents and go to school in Kansas."

"Honestly, Mom, that sounds worse than SBS."

"This is not funny, young man!"

"You're smiling."

"Don't toy with me, Finn Whitman!"

Use of the last name was a red flag. A warning sign. Finn pushed the cereal bowl away, suddenly not hungry.

168

"What do you want me to say? You want me to lie, Mom? Okay! I'll never cross over at night again."

"Do not patronize me, young man!"

"I'm going tonight. Late. Disney Hollywood Studios. There, I didn't lie."

"You are not going."

"I thought you got what we do. The Keepers. My friends. You're a scientist. You build rockets at NASA, Mom!" Finn looked at the clock. "I'm late for school. You're late for work." He stood.

"Sit down!"

Finn obeyed.

"You know there's no scientific explanation for any of this. Your body stays here sleeping while somehow you can think as a hologram at the same time? If I tried to explain that at work, they'd send me to a psychologist."

"He needs us. Wayne needs us."

"It's fantasy, Finn. It's all fantasy."

"The brightest lightning that we see," Finn said, "is from the ground up, not the clouds down. You taught me that. Nothing is as it seems, Mom. Right? Isn't that what you've told me forever? Can I explain this? No. But it happens. Just like the lightning going up, not down. And Wayne's been taken, and he's left us clues to save him and we think we know where to find him."

"Fantasmic!" she said.

"How could you possibly know that?"

"I'm a rocket scientist, remember?"

"Mom?"

"You said you were going late tonight. The only thing in Hollywood Studios late at night is that show."

"Bizarre."

"Logic. Okay. Then you'll go as you, not your hologram."

"What? No! That's not possible."

"It's completely possible."

"It's dangerous. It's more dangerous, Mom."

"Not to me it isn't."

"Nothing hurts our holograms. Almost nothing."

"Finn, tell the others they're not going as holograms. I'll drive."

"No, Mom."

"Yes, Mom," she said. "You go as a normal, healthy boy, or not at all. And you behave yourself."

"Mom, we're the Kingdom Keepers!"

"Not tonight, you aren't. Not again. Not ever again. No more of this sleeping hologram thing or I tell your father."

Finn stared into his mother's eyes, and she into his. *Kansas!* He couldn't focus his thoughts to figure out a way around this. Maybe Philby could think of something.

Or maybe he and the others would throw Finn out of the Keepers for good.

"You've ruined my life."

"Yeah, I'm a real monster."

"No, Mom. I've met real monsters. And you're worse than that."

37

THE OTHERS ALWAYS CREDITED Philby with being the smart one, but Finn had outsmarted his own mother. It was true that Philby made it happen. True, without Philby it couldn't have happened. But Finn had thought it up in the first place.

He and Amanda used the school wrestling room. The sport hadn't been played at his middle school for decades. The room was actually a storage area, but the spongy mat filled the entire floor, making it the most comfortable place to lie down.

He wasn't sure where Maybeck and Jess would "nap." Charlene had said she could find a place at her school to "disappear." And that had been Finn's idea: to disappear. As long as Philby could hack his way into crossing them over, they could enter Hollywood Studios early. Way early. Only thing was, Philby had to do the computer work. He couldn't cross over because he couldn't run a computer in his sleep. He would have to work his magic for the rest of them and then meet them in the Park as his human self. Poor Philby.

By five o'clock that afternoon, Finn had accounted

for every DHI but Philby. With part of his plan involving Wanda's status as Wayne's daughter, Finn and the others met up with her just after sunset at a backstage entrance near the Fantasmic! show.

Finn felt better having everyone together. Hiding in the Park for the long hours between the end of school and sunset had felt like a week. He could picture his mother searching for him everywhere.

He not only had to avoid the Overtakers, but his own mother. Sometimes it was hard to tell the difference.

Wanda led them deeper backstage.

"I brought a friend with me."

"Wayne?" Finn said excitedly.

"No. Don't I wish! Take a look."

She and Finn stopped. She pointed.

"Who the heck?"

Maybeck stood right behind Finn. "That's the dude from outside the Stave Church! Philby and I—"

Wanda interrupted. "I thought he might prove of some benefit to us all." Speaking to the giant Norseman, she said, "Come along now. And do your best to keep up."

Finn, a little dazed, followed Wanda, but couldn't keep from looking over his shoulder at the warrior.

"Fantasmic! is having a tech rehearsal in fifteen

minutes. It's on the Cast Member schedule." Wanda walked like a penguin. "There's a good deal of technology in the Fantasmic! show, including lots of projection. Your DHIs should work fine backstage."

Amanda walked alongside Finn. She asked, "Why would they do a tech rehearsal on a show that's been playing for so long?"

"That's bothering me, too."

"Maybe they do it a lot," she said. She didn't sound confident.

"Maybe Wayne is here somewhere," Finn said, "and messed something up."

"Like a signal."

"Yeah."

"We should find out what part of the show the tech rehearsal is for."

"If we were going to find Wayne, we need to do it now when there's no audience, no danger to them."

"I'm sure you've thought of this." Amanda kept her voice down. "But this show is the perfect place for Maleficent and Chernabog and any villain to hide. I mean if they really are here. So many of them are in this show."

"Wayne says the best place to hide is out in the open."

"Exactly! And that's what they're doing. I mean, if they are really here."

Finn was deep in thought.

"One thing's bugging me," Amanda said. "How could Wayne leave us clues in Epcot to come here? I mean, how could he have known the Overtakers would take him here and not somewhere else?"

"I don't ever try to figure him out. But if I had to guess, I'll bet he was thinking big. He was thinking, if he had green skin or horns, where could he hide without sticking out?"

"So this is some kind of base for the Overtakers?"

"This is the Death Star," Finn said. He let Amanda walk ahead. He drew closer to the Norse warrior, who now carried the Odin sword in place of the plaster one. Only in a place like Disney World could a giant Norse warrior *not* draw weird looks.

"When we get backstage," he told the warrior, "you will stand guard. You will stop anyone dressed like a villain from following us. Do you understand?"

The Norseman nodded.

Finn didn't love being the one in charge. But Wayne had told him from the beginning that he was to be the leader of the Kingdom Keepers.

Finn had been one of the first to cross over while

asleep. He was still the only one who could go all-clear when he wasn't a hologram. Wayne had chosen him. It was that simple. Finn was stuck as leader, like it or not.

"We can do this," he told himself. He rejoined Amanda. Willa and Charlene caught up to them. "Any assignments, Finn?" Willa asked.

"What's the layout?" Finn asked her. Willa was a research freak.

"There's the control booth back there," she said.

"Once Philby gets here—which has probably already happened—he'll take care of that."

"There's seating for several thousand guests. Two acres of water with natural-gas pipes running just under the surface. Those are for the fire effects. About a dozen barges. As you can see," she said, pointing up, "the stage is a mountain. Lots of floors, trapdoors, zip lines, stunt pillows. It's over fifty feet high."

"Backstage?"

"There's a lower level with dressing rooms, equipment storage. Fireworks stuff is loaded-in three hours before every show."

"So everything's happening soon."

"Yes."

"I'll bet the Overtakers wouldn't mind having all those explosives for themselves." Finn saw how dangerous it all was.

"Do you think that's what Wayne discovered?" Willa asked.

"So basically, we're walking into a trap?" Maybeck asked from just behind them.

Finn glanced back. He looked at Maybeck. Their DHIs shimmered, revealing they were on an edge of the projection range. Their DHIs spit static and their skin tone changed. Finn looked a little orange; Maybeck, purple.

"Tech, scene three, thirty seconds," a voice bellowed over a public address system. Wanda stopped backstage at a set of steel stairs.

"I'll stay down here with the warrior," she whispered to Finn. "If you need the sword, I'll get it to you."

"I don't know exactly what we're doing here," Finn said quietly.

"You're looking for my father. You're staying out of trouble. You're going to find him and get him out of here while everyone else is busy."

She made it sound so easy.

A narrator's recorded voice echoed off the empty amphitheater.

Rehearsal had begun.

38

"I'VE GOT YOU SET UP as a stagehand," Wanda whispered to Maybeck. "That way you can wear a headset and hear everything that's going on. Just don't speak into it or they may know you're a fake."

"Seriously?" Maybeck said.

"You'll have full access to everywhere backstage," Wanda said. "You can help Jess search the lower floor for my father."

"If the Overtakers are playing themselves in the show, then we won't know who's real and who's a Cast Member playing a villain. That's risky." Maybeck said it was a risk he didn't think Jess was ready for.

"The hope is that if Jess happens to get close to an Overtaker, she might have one of her flashes, her future visions."

"That seems unlikely," Maybeck said.

Wanda studied him thoughtfully. "Of course it is. And of course it's risky, as you say. But my father is important to this cause. The day will come when you all can do without him. But you are not there yet."

"I get that."

"If Jess is able to see into the future—"

"I said I get it," Maybeck snapped. He apologized immediately. "It's just that Jess and Amanda are new to being DHIs. You've never been one. I am one. Fear weakens us. It's not like they are invincible."

"Understood." Wanda looked distressed. "I don't want anyone hurt."

"Then make sure we work in pairs. And make sure there's a Keeper with both Amanda and Jess. This isn't easy, you know. And it isn't safe."

39

Ms. Whitman knew all the expressions: Be careful what you wish for. And, You can't undo what's already done. Standing outside Lee Middle School with Ms. Philby she hoped it hadn't been a mistake to contact the other parents. She didn't know how much they knew about their children crossing over in their sleep. She didn't want to scare anyone. But Finn had lied. He'd tricked her. She was worried sick.

"Listen," Philby's mother said to her, "I know Dell runs the technology. This crossing over they do. I'm not saying I understand it. Half the time I don't even believe it. But if they've done what you say they've done, then they could be in real trouble."

"Yes."

"I want to do what's right," Ms. Whitman said. "For us. For our children. If we can find them, can figure out what they're up to, maybe we can stop them before something bad happens."

"Am I crazy to believe that when Dell goes to sleep he becomes a hologram in the Parks?" Philby's mother was a slight woman with oversized eyes and an expressive face. Ms. Philby looked dazed. "I don't know what to believe."

"Not everything can be explained," Ms. Whitman said. "I'm a scientist by training."

"You work for NASA."

"That's right. And I continue to see things in space exploration that defy our models of understanding. Maybe there is pixie dust. Maybe there is magic. I don't know. What I do know is that our children believe in all this. Real or not, that puts them at risk. Great risk."

"Why take such risks?" Philby's mom looked ready to cry.

"The children believe Wayne Kresky has been kidnapped," Ms. Whitman said, leaving out the role of the Overtakers. "I think they've gone to the Park to save him."

"They're good kids," Philby's mom said, sniffling.

"I know it sounds—"

"Ridiculous? Absurd? Impossible?" Ms. Philby was losing her patience. "Yes, it does!"

Ms. Whitman felt a headache coming on. "I understand it sounds crazy," she muttered. "I think they're here in the school. I think they're asleep here in school. I think they're holograms."

"Maybe not Dell. I think he's the one who controls the technology."

"Finn is inside. We won't be able to wake him up." Ms. Whitman crossed her arms nervously.

"Well then, let's find out if you're right. And if you are, we find their holograms," Ms. Philby said.

"You understand we are breaking into a school?"

"Yes," Ms. Philby said. "And if we find any of them, we don't touch them. We don't disturb them. We get back in the car and we find their holograms and tell them to stop this, this instant!"

"Agreed." Ms. Whitman reached into her purse and produced a small pry bar. She held it up for Philby's mom to see. She smiled.

Ten minutes later they were shining their mobile phone flashlights onto two children asleep in a wrestling room.

"This is terrifying," Ms. Philby choked out. "They look—"

"Don't say it!" Ms. Whitman drew a deep breath. Finn's body was right there only a few feet away. "I think I know which park they're in."

"Their holograms."

"Yes."

"Then what are we waiting for?"

40

PHILBY—NOT HIS HOLOGRAM, but the real boy—
stood behind the Fantasmic! control booth. The amphitheater was empty. There was a sound check or something going on. He couldn't walk through walls. He
couldn't poke his head through the door to see what was
going on.

Instead, he knocked once sharply. "Hey!" he called
through the door. "Radios are down. You're wanted
backstage." He slipped into a row of bench seats
and squatted.

The Cast Member inside the show control opened
the door. Seeing no one, she took off in a hurry toward
the stage, mumbling to herself angrily.

Philby caught the door before it locked shut. He
stepped inside. He faced a sound mixing board, a light
board, and another board the purpose of which was
unknown to him. The walls of the tiny cinder block
booth held shelves cluttered with computer parts.

He sat down at the controls. The boards were com-
puterized. An array of screens showed several views
of various locations on the stage. Another carried the

run-of-show menu. It listed in order every light and sound cue for the show. Only then did the purpose of the third board make sense: pyrotechnics. It was the fireworks controller.

Philby slipped on the headset resting on the console.

"Okay," Philby heard someone say. "We made it through scene three without a glitch. Let's keep running the show and hope that's all we needed to do. Control, scene four."

The technician he tricked wouldn't be gone long. Philby pressed the button attached to the headset. He said, "Roll scene four." He clicked a mouse on the screen where a "button" was marked SCENE 4. The menu scrolled. The programmed slides on the sound and light control boards moved independently. Philby ran the boards for his school theater productions. He took a moment to make sure the door to the booth was locked. He felt right at home.

41

WANDA LEFT CHARLENE, Amanda, and Finn tucked into some bushes near the backstage entrance to the Fantasmic! stage. Hiding a plaster Norse warrior was more difficult. Finn spotted a large electrical transformer away from backstage and told the warrior to go hide there and wait. "Once I'm inside, I'm going to need the sword. And maybe some protection. If any of us ask you for the sword, you give it." The warrior grunted and marched off.

Rising above the three, the structure looked like an oil-rig platform. The back of the stage set was not made to look like a mountain. Instead, a series of open concrete platforms, protected by steel-pipe railings rose at least fifty feet into the ever-darkening sky. There was only the one backstage entrance. Though presently unguarded, something warned Finn not to enter.

He felt something, someone guiding him. Wayne? His own sixth sense? He wasn't sure. But the feeling was strong. If he and the girls used the entrance, they'd be caught.

"We need a different way in," he said.

Charlene studied the various platforms backstage. Her head spun as she looked into the empty amphitheater. "Okay," she said. "I think I've got something."

"What?"

"Not going to say. I'm not going to get us all caught. If it works, then follow me. If it doesn't, then—" She grinned ironically. Not exactly a smile of happiness.

"No, Charlie," Amanda said.

Charlene held that weird smile as she seemed to be talking to herself. But she wasn't. "You two do what needs to be done to find and rescue Wayne. Promise me you'll do that first and come for me later." An aching silence between them. "Promise me."

"I can't do that," Finn said.

"You know what, Finn? You are so predictable!"

Charlene slipped out of the bushes and took off running. Finn reached for her arm but missed.

"This is not good," Finn said.

Amanda grabbed onto his arm. "She's the fastest, most athletic of all of you. I wouldn't want to try to catch her."

He wanted to call Charlene back. To stop her before either Park Security or an Overtaker did. But she'd timed it well. A voice said over the speakers, "Roll scene four." Not just any voice.

"That's Philby," Finn whispered secretively.

"Look!" Amanda said, turning his chin in Charlene's direction.

Charlene had spun around. She was running backward!

She was looking at Finn and Amanda.

"She is so busted," Finn said.

"It's a diversion. She wants to be seen! She wants us to sneak backstage with the attention all on her." Of all things, Amanda sounded . . . envious.

"She's smarter than that," Finn said. "At least I hope she is."

Charlene disappeared.

Vanished.

She was gone from sight. One moment running backward. The next, poof!

Amanda squeezed Finn's arm again. He was going to bruise.

"That's DHI shadow, right?" Amanda said softly.

"What the fudge?" Finn stammered. "Projectors! She wasn't checking out the stage. She was looking for DHI projectors. There's a DHI shadow between the waterway and the front of the stage."

"If we make ourselves invisible, we can sneak

backstage," Amanda said. "How smart of her." She stared at Finn as if waiting for his reaction.

Finn didn't know if he should look impressed with Charlene, or act like it meant nothing to him. "Yeah," he said. "Right. So, let's go."

42

In hiding backstage, Finn, Charlene, and Amanda watched the stagehands who were busy with the tech rehearsal. The work continued thanks to Philby. Finn's plan was to get into position prior to Maleficent's appearance near the end of the show. Villains' faces would transform on screens into Chernabog. An explosion of flames would leave Maleficent on stage alone. Before she conjured the dragon, before Mickey battled the dragon, Finn would strike with Odin's sword.

The Keepers had fought Maleficent plenty of times. Finn would be able to see the difference between a Cast Member playing the dark fairy and the real thing.

Charlene was going to try to trap Chernabog. If they locked him up, then the demon couldn't go on whatever trip Chef and Mabel had planned for him.

The current issue facing Finn, Amanda, and Charlene was the large number of villains—Overtakers—in the show. They would be backstage. Any of them could be dangerous! They also might be nothing but Cast Members. How to know the difference?

Timing was everything.

"I'm going to scout the upper platforms," Charlene said, already climbing up the stage wall. "Wait here."

Alone with Amanda, Finn felt awkward. He worked through his plan in his head, trying to memorize everything there was to do. Amanda spoke.

"You're taking Mickey's place in the show," she said. "Did I hear that right?"

"Yes. I'll wear the Mickey costume."

"But isn't that risky, Finn?" she asked.

"Maleficent is only on stage for a minute. It's the only chance I'll have."

Amanda clearly didn't like Finn's answer. "Mickey overpowers Maleficent with his mind, Finn, not a sword."

"Wayne wanted us—me—to have Odin's sword. There's a reason for that."

"Sometimes things are really simple, Finn. There are more of them than us. We're outnumbered. Maleficent and Chernabog are not just powerful, they are darkly powerful. They've been trying to kill you guys since the Magic Kingdom. What part of this makes sense to you?"

Finn wasn't sure what to say. Amanda was worried for him. In his whole life only his parents had looked at him like Amanda was looking at him.

"I'll be fine," he said.

"That's not necessarily true. Maybe you won't be," Amanda said. "Girls know this kind of stuff better than boys, Finn." Amanda sounded so sure of herself. "You're being stupid. I don't like you when you're stupid, when you do stupid things. How am I supposed to like you?"

"Do you? Like me?" Finn's chest hurt.

"I didn't say that." Amanda blushed.

"But I thought—"

"You thought wrong. Being worried about a friend and liking him are two different things."

He didn't understand any of what she was saying. Maybe he was being stupid. He certainly felt stupid.

"There," Amanda said. Charlene was waving from a higher platform. "She's in position. Now's your chance to play hero."

"It's not like that, Amanda."

"Some heroes are dead heroes, Finn. If that happens to you, I am going to be so mad."

"Mad, not sad?"

"Shut up."

Finn was taken aback. "Not cool. You've never told me to shut up before."

"Yeah? Well you've never been quite this stupid. I guess there's a first time for everything."

"Amanda! Come on! This is you and me!" He tried to make eye contact with her, but her eyes were dark and cold.

"If you do this, there is no you and me."

43

FINN'S MOM PARKED HER CAR on a dark, tree-lined road. Just beyond the trees stretched a tall chain link fence.

"This is the back side of Epcot," Ms. Philby said.

"Yes, as it happens." Ms. Whitman turned off the car engine. She looked straight out the windshield, not at her passenger. "They're at the Fantasmic! show."

"It's early for that. Why are you waiting? Let's get into the Park and find them."

"Fantasmic! doesn't open for another hour at least. No one's going to let us in there."

"I'm still not understanding."

"It's dark. But directly through there . . ." Finn's mom said, pointing out the passenger window. Ms. Philby leaned back to avoid being stabbed.

"You are not suggesting we climb the fence and sneak onto Disney property, are you?" Ms. Philby sounded terrified. "That's illegal. That is wrong for so many reasons."

"That's how we get backstage at Fantasmic! That's the only way. Our other choice is to go the proper way, through the Park entrance and stand in a waiting line for the show. Even once we get in, no one is going to let us backstage. We need to get backstage, Gladis. Our children are backstage."

"I'm not getting arrested." She sounded definite.

"I can do this alone," Finn's mom said. "You can stay here and be my scout. Warn me if you see anything suspicious."

"Like a woman my age sneaking around backstage at Hollywood Studios?"

"Exactly like that," Ms. Whitman said.

"I'm coming with you."

"I thought so."

"I haven't done anything like this since my junior year in college. We pulled a sorority prank on a fraternity down the row. Ansel Spratt. Cutest guy I'd seen. Only reason I went along with it was the chance to see Ansel."

"How'd it work out?"

"Best night of college. Best night ever." Ms. Philby smiled.

"See? We're going to have fun."

"No," Ms. Philby said. "We're going to get arrested. Our children are going to disown us. We'll need lawyers."

"Like I said: fun."

44

FINN HEARD THE SCUFFLE of feet and went rigid. He and Amanda ducked into hiding as two stagehands approached and walked past.

Finn held his breath.

The stagehands disappeared down a staircase.

Amanda hadn't spoken for several minutes.

"You're mad at me."

"It's too dangerous, Finn. You and the real Maleficent out there on stage? Maybe the most powerful dark fairy ever. How's that going to work out?" She hesitated. "I thought we were trying to find Wayne. What happened to that plan?"

"That's what we're doing. He gave us the paper box. He wanted us to find Odin's sword. He wanted me here to fight Maleficent if necessary."

"We don't know that. All I'm asking is for you to let me be near you when you're on stage. I can push if you need help."

"Like you did at Expedition Everest."

Amanda had saved Finn's life inside Everest. He had thanked her right after. They'd never discussed it since.

"I'll have the sword," he said. "We didn't face a fire-breathing dragon in Expedition Everest."

"You trust that piece of plaster to bring you the sword?"

"I do. And I trust Jess to sense if it's the real Maleficent I'm facing."

"You don't have to worry about that, Finn. Maleficent had her under that spell for a long time. A very long time. She and Jess are connected now. If Maleficent is anywhere around here, Jess will know it. I have no doubts about that. Zero."

"We're trusting her."

"And you're trusting a plaster statue. But you don't trust me."

"It's not like that, Amanda."

The look she gave Finn could have turned him to plaster.

196

45

Philby only had a few minutes before the show's technician would return. If she caught him inside the control booth, the stage manager would probably cancel both the rehearsal and the real show for security reasons. The Keepers would fail.

Philby moved the computer mouse and worked the keyboard. His assignment was to edit the order and timing of Maleficent's scenes. He had to give Finn enough time to fight the dark fairy before she turned into the dragon.

Maleficent wouldn't know Philby had changed things. Finn would. It would provide a slight advantage. A fighting chance.

46

BACKSTAGE WAS A LABYRINTH of hallways and staircases.

"You okay?" Amanda asked.

"Been better," Finn said.

"This is only going to work if you and Charlene time it right," she said.

"I know that."

"Look, count on Willa finding Mickey's costume. She'll warn the Cast Member playing him. Cast Members love you guys—the Keepers. Because of that, they will believe her."

"I like your sudden optimism."

"I'm trying to stay positive."

"It's working," he said. He felt his hands shaking. He hid them so she wouldn't see.

Over the sound system, he heard the mirror talking to the Evil Queen.

". . . in Mickey's imagination, beauty and love will always survive."

"Beauty and love! Did you hear that?" Amanda asked.

"Yeah."

Maleficent would be on the stage soon. Where was the costume? Where was the sword? Had Philby slowed down the show to give Finn more time on stage? More time to expose and defeat Maleficent?

47

GLADIS PHILBY DROPPED from the Park side of the chain link fence. The ground was damp and soft. It smelled earthy and dank, like clothes left in the washing machine overnight.

"Stay low. Don't let them see us." Ms. Whitman breathed hard and fast.

"I'm not exactly the yoga type."

"Once we're there we'll split up. All we are doing is observing. Make sure your phone is on vibrate. We'll text if we see them. No matter what, we can't be seen or heard."

"Okay. You sound like you've done this before."

"Not really."

"I'm not sure I wanted to know that."

"Sometimes you have to save kids from themselves."

"Dell is hereby grounded for life."

The women started off through the field of tall grass. The lights of Fantasmic! drew ever closer.

48

JESS DID NOT WANT TO BE HERE. Backstage offered only a maze of hallways and staircases. In low light her DHI glowed, making her worried she'd be spotted as someone who didn't belong.

Every so often she paused. She closed her eyes. She tried to feel the way she felt when going to sleep. Peaceful. Quiet. She searched her feelings for Maleficent. It was like holding up a mobile phone to get a better signal.

She understood the risks of her efforts. Maleficent was no one to mess with. Jess had once lived as a captive of her dark magic. She knew the depth of the Dark Fairy's evil ways, the gravitational pull of her spells.

Jess felt like she had swallowed worms. Maleficent believed Jess's ability to see the future to be a threat.

Do not underestimate her! Jess swore to herself.

In that instant, like a flick of a wand, she felt an eerie cold invade her. An animal had crawled inside her skin and was looking for a way out.

It was she: the Dark Fairy.

At once, images flashed in front of Jess. She saw

colors in the sky. An airplane. A man wearing a beret. She saw a strange-looking Mickey Mouse with anime eyes. Maleficent grinned. Finn was there, conducting an orchestra. Maybeck and Wayne!

Too excited by the sight of Wayne, Jess lost her vision. She steadied herself.

She squinted and threw herself back into the nightmare vision. Chernabog's half-bull, half-human face was all she could see. His breath smelled like a trash can left in the summer sun. She blinked. Held her eyes open.

She stopped the vision. She found herself standing in the same lower-level hallway beneath Fantasmic!

Maleficent is here, she thought. She's close.

Jess was not used to being a hologram. She felt her fear of Maleficent change her. The Keepers had warned her and Amanda of the change. If you lose your DHI then you can be hurt. Your hologram goes solid.

If anything was going to turn her solid it was Chernabog and Maleficent.

A door swung open down the corridor. Jess stepped back. A person came out into the hallway. No, not a person. It wore a black robe with purple trim.

Below the trim Jess saw green skin. The air grew cold!

"You there!" Maleficent's familiar voice called out. She didn't recognize Jess. Maybe it was because of Jess's brown hair. Maybe the dark fairy just didn't expect Jess to be standing a few feet away at Fantasmic!

A voice like breaking ice. "I'm due on stage. Are you the one taking me? Where is Annie?"

Afraid Maleficent might recognize Jess's voice, the girl said nothing.

"Answer me! I need you to throw the switch on the elevator. It operates from the outside. I hate rehearsals!"

Jess affected her voice to disguise it. "Yes, ma'am. The switch."

"Well, hurry it up! I'm late!" Maleficent turned and strolled down the hall. Jess caught up. The air turned intensely cold.

Jess had no doubt this was the real Maleficent.

She had to tell Willa!

Jess followed the icy creature. By now, Finn would be on an upper stage waiting for Maleficent's arrival.

Waiting to defeat it.

49

CHARLENE FOUND A LONG length of pirate chain. Attached to it was a large padlock with a key sticking out. The chain was next to some bows and arrows and a coil of rope. The thing was impossibly heavy and cumbersome. Charlene hung it around her shoulders.

There was no time to waste. She took hold of the ladder rising toward one of the stages overhead. She began to climb.

In the midst of her climb she heard voices. She looked down onto the heads of two men.

"Do you think they'll fix the problem?" one of them said.

"Have to find it first. No. It's like a typical glitch, you ask me. We can't make it happen when we want to fix it, but we can't stop it from happening either."

"What are we supposed to do about it?"

"No clue. How do you fix a problem you can't find?"

Charlene couldn't move. The chain would make

noise. The men would see her, barely two feet above their heads.

She was trapped.

Finn needed her.

What now?

50

WEARING A CAST MEMBER Security guard uniform that was too small for him, Maybeck watched from offstage as the Evil Queen turned into the Hag. A bubbling cauldron appeared in front of her. She called out for "the forces of evil" to turn the dream into "a nightmare Fantasmic!"

Maybeck shuddered. The expression seemed like something an Overtaker would say. Turn a dream into a nightmare.

It seemed obvious to him. He and the Keepers had figured out Wayne's message correctly. Whatever happened here in the next few minutes was important. To the Parks. To the good magic. To the Kingdom Keepers.

He heard a commotion below. He leaned to look over the outside railing.

The Norse warrior had just knocked two Cast Members onto the ground. He was marching toward the stairs, the sword held before him.

51

MONITORING THE VARIOUS screens showing views from stage cameras, Philby slipped out of the control room only seconds before the technicians returned.

He'd successfully changed the show's timeline. He'd blocked Mickey's trapdoor lift. He'd delayed Maleficent's flashy exit. Philby had no control over what Finn might do, but he'd given him time to do it. The rest was up to Finn.

52

MALEFICENT STEPPED INTO the elevator lift. Jess kept her head down staring at the lift's control box. It contained three oversized buttons: UP, DOWN, and EMERGENCY STOP.

Maleficent pulled her robes tightly around her. She was supposed to go up into the blinding spotlight on the stage. She would take the place of the Hag. The actor playing the Hag would then come down the same lift.

A small light flashed green. That was the signal. Jess was about to send Maleficent up to fight Finn. Her friend. Amanda's friend. The leader of the Kingdom Keepers. It seemed so wrong to do such a thing. Her finger shook as it pointed at the large UP button.

"Push it, you fool!" said Maleficent. "The green light! That's my—"

Jess had made the mistake of looking up at the dark fairy.

"Jess?" Maleficent's voice cracked. Always so calm, Jess thought. Always so cool—cold!—and in control. But in that instant Maleficent was both shocked and surprised.

Jess grinned maliciously. She triggered the lift to rise.

"Jess?" Again. This time, more desperate.

Maleficent never showed fear.

"You? How?" the Dark Fairy gasped dryly, now out of sight.

"Me," Jess said.

53

A Roman soldier just passed a sword to a girl who might have been Charlene.

Ms. Whitman read the text. It didn't make sense to her. She wrote back.

I haven't seen any of them. Charlene?

I think it was Charlene. She took the sword up a ladder with her. The soldier hurt a couple stagehands.

The boys?

No. Haven't seen them so far.

I'm going to get closer. You stay put. OK?

Ms. Whitman received a thumbs-up Tapback. She caught movement out of the corner of her eye. It came from the amphitheater's empty bleachers. She looked more closely, scanning the endless benches rising from the water tank high up the incline.

A boy's head appeared. He was tucked down into the empty benches. He was clearly in hiding.

I see Philby! she typed. **That's it! I'm going in!**

54

A BURST OF FLAMES ERUPTED. Maleficent appeared on stage. A coil of smoke twisted and rose like a hand with long fingers.

Wearing the Mickey suit and covering Odin's sword with a swath of his cape, Finn stood slightly offstage, awaiting his entrance. He spotted a stagehand holding back a small man shaking his fist at Finn. The man was visibly upset. He had to be the Cast Member who was supposed to be playing Mickey.

"He's an imposter!" the Cast Member said.

The stagehand shushed the man.

If Finn didn't hurry the whole plan would be ruined. Finn had no time to weigh options. No time to make sure he wouldn't be put under a spell by Maleficent or crushed by Chernabog or burned to a crisp by the dragon.

He stepped out onto the stage.

Maleficent turned toward him. Finn pulled out the sword. He held it at his side.

Behind Maleficent and offstage, a figure ran into the wings. It was Jess. She looked directly at Mickey/Finn and nodded.

The dark fairy facing Finn was the real Maleficent, not a Cast Member playing her.

"It's you, isn't it, boy?" Maleficent said. Her amplified voice sang out loud and powerful. It echoed into the empty amphitheater.

By going off script, Maleficent won the full attention of all the stagehands.

"Wrong line!" A woman reading from a loose-leaf notebook turned pages quickly.

Finn hoped Charlene was in place. He counted on Philby to have changed the timing of the dragon's fire. Finn took another step closer to Maleficent. Odin's sword felt heavy.

"You attacked us in Epcot," he said. "You lost. We know you have Wayne. He led us here." With Jess standing close by, the idea was to make Maleficent think of Wayne. The hope was that Jess might "see" what Maleficent was thinking. Maybe she would lead them to Wayne.

"Impossible."

"Wayne is not a dark fairy or a monster. He's not a demon or a witch. Yet, here we are. He's a hero, something you will never be."

Finn stole a glance at Jess. Eyes closed. Chin down. She emitted an intensity. She was trying to link up with Maleficent. To see what she saw.

The plan was in place. Finn was supposed to upset Maleficent. He hoped to make her step away from the cauldron and toward Finn.

Stagehands were busy in the wings. They couldn't figure out why both Mickey and Maleficent had gone off script.

Finn raised his sword. If all else failed, he would use it on her. He took two steps toward Maleficent. His action encouraged the dark fairy to close the distance. Finn stepped onto the square pattern in the stage flooring. One of several trapdoors.

Any second now.

55

PHILBY CHECKED HIS PHONE. He had a good signal where he was kneeling between benches in the amphitheater. He double-checked the phone's web browser. The address bar showed a series of letters, numbers, colons, and forward slashes.

One push of a button and his phone would hack the control booth. At first, the Cast Member inside wouldn't understand what was happening. But she was probably extremely smart. As Philby manipulated the show she would work to take back control. Philby would have control for a minute at the most. At that point the show runner would unlink the control panels from the Internet.

Philby watched and listened to the standoff between Maleficent and Finn. It didn't seem to be going well for Finn.

His finger hovered over his phone.

He pushed the button.

56

FINN COULDN'T IMAGINE he would actually strike Maleficent with the sword. The idea of that repulsed him. Threaten her? Absolutely. But he was no killer. He would leave that to others.

He stepped off the trapdoor and moved to the side, keeping the steaming cauldron between himself and Maleficent. Hopefully, Philby had done his job.

"You silly, silly boy," she said. "Do you actually believe a few children have any sort of chance against our powers?" She waved a hand and the cauldron tipped over, spilling steaming green goo at Finn's feet.

Finn jumped out of the way. The cauldron was a stage prop. It should not have had anything in it. She filled the caldron with a spell! Finn thought.

The dark fairy opened her hand. A fireball appeared. It spit sparks loudly. Smoke rose from her hand. She felt nothing.

She launched the burning ball at Finn. He raised the sword and knocked it away. The ball flew into the wings of the stage and exploded. The sound of fire extinguishers hissed as stagehands fought the flames.

A stagehand shouted, "Loretta, what's going on? Rehearsal's over. That's it! Done!"

She threw a second fireball at the stagehand. He ducked and ran offstage.

"Did you know the new version of Fantasmic! includes the defeat of the Kingdom Keepers? I'm a movie star now. I get what I want."

She waved. A cage of burning beams enclosed Finn. He was trapped.

"See, boy? This is how you lose. This is all new material."

57

FINN WALKED HIS DHI TO the burning bars believing his hologram—dressed in the Mickey costume—would keep him safe. He burned his arm and jumped back.

Maleficent cackled with laughter. She was loving this. She waved her arms again. The burning cage began shrinking in on Finn.

It would all be over quickly for Finn if he didn't do something fast. He took a calming breath. He pictured a dark tunnel with only a pinprick of light at the end. In his imagination, he moved in the direction of the light. The sword fell from his hand as he went all-clear.

Finn stepped through the burning bars. The Mickey costume was fire resistant. It singed black in a few places but did not catch fire.

Maleficent snarled unhappily. Her eyes rolled back in her head.

The sword was trapped inside the cage. He wondered what was holding up Philby. Things weren't exactly going to plan.

Maleficent raised her arm.

BOOM! A blinding flash of white light preceded a dazzling wash of fog and smoke that rose high into the sky revealing . . . Chernabog. It was her spell, her show now—no longer Fantasmic! She had summoned the demon instead of the dragon.

Finn was in trouble.

The demon only made himself visible for a matter of seconds. The image seared itself into Finn's brain.

The next flash of light caught Maleficent by surprise. She clearly had not been expecting this.

Philby? Finn wondered.

Chernabog vanished. The massive dragon took his place. Not the four-story puppet dragon Finn had expected. Not the dragon Philby was supposed to now be controlling.

This dragon's flesh shined. Muscles flexed as it swung its long neck.

It was a real dragon.

58

CHARLENE'S JOB WAS TO monitor the dragon. The Animatronic dragon. If everything had worked to plan, Philby's changes would have caused the beast to spit his fire onto Maleficent. She was supposed to go up in flames.

But this wasn't that dragon. It was Maleficent's. It was real! Everything was wrong. She saw that Finn couldn't possibly fight both Maleficent and the dragon at the same time.

Maleficent threw another fireball at Finn. It passed right through his DHI without harming him.

"Old green fairies are no longer needed here," he said. He moved off the trapdoor. He looked up at Charlene.

Do something! Finn's eyes pleaded.

"Little children should know their place," Maleficent scolded him.

The dark fairy raised her arm, signaling the dragon.

The dragon craned its huge head toward Finn. Its red eyes blinked. It opened its jaws. It moved its heavy feet.

Finn charged Maleficent. He took hold of her

raised arm. He stopped her from signaling the dragon to unleash more fire.

Her arm was so cold that his hand stuck to her green skin. He'd lost his all-clear!

Frightened, he released her arm. Feathers were growing out of it. Her face elongated. Her skin turned brown. Her pointy nose stretched and hardened into a long beak. A flap of skin appeared under her jaw. She was transfiguring into a hideous vulture.

Finn slammed into her. He knocked her back.

Maleficent banged into the spilled cauldron. Her right wing touched the green goo. The feathers dissolved.

From beneath her, one of the vulture's talons shot out and shoved Finn's DHI across the stage.

The giant bird rose to its feet. Its wings extended. It was a foul-looking thing. Its head was bald, its beak hooked. Finn clambered to his feet, eyes searching for the trapdoor.

The dragon was leaning off its perch. The vulture cawed at the dragon. Another Maleficent command.

Finn was going to burn.

"Philby!" he shouted, his voice booming through the speakers.

As the beast's chest swelled, Charlene understood the dragon was going to set Finn on fire.

Finn's going to die! she thought.

She took hold of one end of the chain. She dragged it behind as she jumped onto the dragon's foot.

She bent and looped the chain around the dragon's ankle. She nearly had the chain locked to itself as the beast shook her off.

Charlene flew like a bug. But she held on to the chain. She swung out and around the dragon ankle a second time. As she smashed onto its slippery skin, she turned the key.

The angry dragon tried again to shake her off. It lost its balance, scrambled back. But with one ankle chained, it staggered off balance.

Charlene stood. She needed to jump off before the dragon crushed her.

She caught sight of a small pile of props. It included bows and arrows and four or five spears. She grabbed one of the spears. She looked up at the dragon. Yes, she could throw the spear. Yes, she could probably hit the dragon's neck. But would a small spear in the neck help? What if it just made the creature angry and mean?

She'd read a good series of books on the world of Greek mythology.

Achilles.

His mother, Thetis, had dipped him in the river Styx to make him immortal. But since she had held him by one heel to dunk him, this one part of his body had remained dry. That spot, the back of his heel, made him vulnerable. Achilles's heel.

She slashed down into the back of the dragon's ankle. It was like trying to cut a thick rope. The dragon roared. Charlene moved the sharp blade of the spear like a knife. Something snapped. It sounded like a loud clap.

She'd never heard anything like what came next: a roaring mixture of pain and fire.

59

THE NORSE WARRIOR had sworn allegiance to Philby and Maybeck. It didn't mean much to either of the boys until Maybeck saw the plaster giant marching toward him at the side of the main stage. His joints were all cracked. Plaster dust fell from them. His beard looked like it might fall off. His eyes looked determined.

With the show going wrong, the stagehands had scattered. Maybeck stood in the wings watching the standoff between Finn and Maleficent. As Charlene attacked the dragon, he feared she was about to die.

He felt paralyzed, unsure what to do.

The warrior stopped a matter of feet from Maybeck. Stood there like a soldier awaiting orders.

A chunk of plaster.

60

FINN BACKED UP AS THE vulture moved toward him. He'd left the trapdoor. No escape. He would have to stay and fight.

About to fry Finn to death, the dragon's head had turned. It roared fire into the sky. It tried to walk, but stumbled, its head slamming the stage.

And there was Charlene. A spear in hand.

Maleficent, now a vulture, thrust her beak at Finn's head.

He stole a look at Odin's sword. It lay on the stage in the middle of the burning cage.

"You and me," Finn said to the vulture/Maleficent. He looked into the bird's hideous eyes. The vulture advanced another step. Her pink tongue slipped through her beak like a snake's.

"It's over." Not his voice. Not hers.

The voice was older. Deeper. The voice of an old man. Then Finn identified it. Wayne's voice.

High above the stage on an outcropping of rock stood Wayne in his khaki pants. His white hair blew in the wind. He wore an Epcot windbreaker.

He looked exactly as Jess had dreamed him.

Wayne called down. "We've lost, Finn. It's over. Surrender is the only option."

"No!" Finn shouted.

"Listen to him!" The vulture could speak. It croaked in a grating voice. "He's trying to help you!"

"No!" Finn said, continuing to move away from the trapdoor. "You've put a spell on him!"

"Save yourself," Wayne called down.

"Finn!" He knew that voice as well. Amanda! She stood alongside Maybeck. The Norse warrior looked on as well. What's he doing here? Finn wondered.

"Don't you dare surrender!" Amanda called out. "End her, or I will!" She lifted her hands, palms out.

The vulture pivoted, raised her wings as if to fly.

Amanda *pushed* with both hands.

Finn expected the vulture to lift. Maybe it would use Amanda's force against the girl. Catch the force in its wings and fly high.

But the vulture didn't move.

A scraping sound. Finn looked in time to see the sword sliding through the burning bars of the cage. Amanda hadn't pushed the vulture. She'd pushed the sword to Finn!

Maleficent, the vulture, saw what Amanda had done. The bird spun and lunged at Finn, its beak outthrust.

He clenched his hands around the sword's grip and hoisted the blade, aiming it between him and the vulture. The tip pierced the bird's feathers. The vulture shrieked and cried out. Thick green fluid oozed from under her wing.

As Finn withdrew the blade, the vulture shrank and contracted. It reformed into the green-faced dark fairy of Maleficent. She carried the wound below her left arm.

She staggered.

"Burn him!" she hollered, covering her wound with a bony hand.

The dragon roared.

Finn caught motion to his right. The Norse warrior marched toward Finn in long strides. His feet clunked across the stage.

The warrior stepped in front of Finn just as the dragon released its molten wind. Fire flowed from its gaping mouth, the stream of fire aimed directly at Finn. The plaster warrior acted as a shield, deflecting the flame around him and the boy who stood behind. Finn was protected.

The warrior turned a violent red. As he absorbed the extraordinary heat, he began to glow like a charcoal ember. Pieces and chunks of plaster turned to ash and fell from the statue. The dragon fire stopped. The warrior broke apart entirely, a pile of ash at Finn's feet.

Several stage level trapdoors opened at once. But Finn was not standing on one.

It wasn't him who fell through to safety. The wounded Maleficent vanished.

Finn dropped to his knees. The dragon wasn't finished. It unleased fire onto Wayne, high atop the mountain. Fire swallowed Wayne in a coil of blue-and-orange flame.

When the fire stopped, Wayne was gone.

Finn screamed.

The dragon teetered, unable to set down its wounded foot. It hopped, lost its balance, and fell over the wall and off the mountaintop. A length of thick chain followed from its wounded foot. A loud thud filled the air. And then, silence.

Charlene stood, rising from where the beast had been. Amanda ran across the stage, leaping over two open trapdoors, and slid to Finn's side.

She threw her arms around him.

Finn dropped the sword and hugged her. "He saved my life," he said. The pile of ash still glowed red.

"You saved us all," she whispered.

61

THE KEEPERS MET UP at Soundstage B on the Hollywood Studios backlot. Ms. Philby and Finn's mom were there with them. The moms did their best to console Wanda, distraught over Wayne's loss.

The Park had suffered power outages following the rehearsal. The evening's performance of Fantasmic! had been canceled. The six holograms flickered due to the power problems. Only Philby, who wasn't a hologram, looked like himself.

"I'm sorry," Finn said, apologizing to all. "I don't know how I lost it." In all the confusion Finn could not find the Return fob.

"I'll figure it out," Philby said. He sat at a computer terminal in the corner of the lounge, his fingers busy on the keyboard. "There must be a way I can make the server Return you all. Wayne couldn't have designed the DHI system with only one fob."

"I have a copy of his office key," Wanda said, wiping away her tears. "He has—had—an office here on the property. The management offices. Maybe there's something there that will help."

Willa accepted the key. "Thanks. I'll go look." She headed out.

Finn said, "He was a good man. A great man."

"No kidding," said Charlene.

Wanda nodded solemnly. "I know he wouldn't want me crying over him," she said. "But I'm going to miss him so much. I'm going to head home now. But please contact me if you need me."

Finn tried to hug her, but his hologram was all-clear. Thankfully, his effort made Wanda smile.

The two moms offered to drive Wanda home and she agreed. Finn caught his mom's concerned eye.

"I'll be home soon," he said.

"You'd better be," she said. "I'm going to be waiting by your bed. Waiting for you to wake up."

Finn thought his heart might explode in his chest. In his mind's eye he saw Wayne sitting next to him on a bench in the Magic Kingdom. He saw Wayne climbing Escher's Keep. He recalled the sparkle in the man's eyes and the calm in his voice. The memories that would not soon fade.

"He taught us," Finn said. "He changed us."

"He loved these Parks," said Philby.

"We're all going to miss him," said Maybeck.

Finn wasn't sure how long they stayed like that. Maybeck told a story about Wayne in Magic Kingdom.

Wanda came back from Wayne's office with a Return fob. The Keepers could be back home in bed with the push of a button. None of them wanted to leave.

Wanda's grief overcame her once again. She apologized for leaving but had to get home. There were hologram hugs all around. Wanda left.

62

THE SUN ROSE ABOVE Hollywood Studios. Cast Members would be arriving soon. The soundstage would not be safe for them much longer.

Finn held up the fob Willa had found. "Is everyone ready to go home?"

"No!" Philby called from the soundstage control room. He was in there at a computer.

"What's with him?" Maybeck asked.

Willa explained. "He's been replaying the Fantasmic! rehearsal videos. He can't let it go, can't accept that we lost Wayne."

"We can't go yet," Philby called.

"We've got to get back, Philby. Especially you. We're all DHIs. You're not."

"'Beware your friends and know your enemies,'" Philby said, quoting Wayne.

The group moved to the control room door and looked in on Philby.

"Come on, Philby. Give it a rest," Maybeck said.

"We're all tired. It's been a long night," Finn said.

"Wayne was the traitor," Philby said.

He silenced the others. A tension filled the air.

"Don't say stuff like that," Finn chided.

"Think about it," Philby said. "Why would Wayne tell us to surrender?"

"I was going to be killed," Finn said.

"You're missing the point. Wayne would never tell us to surrender. Not ever."

"We all saw him, Philby," Maybeck said. "We heard him."

Willa said, "Just like we saw Maleficent vanish through a trapdoor."

"I saw the dragon fall," Charlene said. "And I saw it getting tied up down on the ground. It was hurt, but not dead."

Philby said, "Being DHIs has taught us that we can't always trust what we see. Right? I mean . . . look, you guys! Are you real?"

"You need some sleep," Maybeck said. "We all do. We've got to hit the button and Return. Right now."

"Shadows," Philby said.

"You're tired," Maybeck said. "You're upset. It wasn't your fault, Philby. It wasn't any of our faults."

Philby turned the computer screen around for all to see. "Check it out," he said. He rewound the video footage of the battle on the Fantasmic! stage. "Willa!" he said, handing her his cell phone, its flashlight app turned on. "Look at Maleficent's vulture. What do you see?" Philby asked.

"She's ugly?" Charlene said.

"Big?" Maybeck said.

"Terrifying," said Finn.

Philby pointed to the screen. "Shadows. The stage lights throw shadows."

"Duh," Maybeck said.

"Check out Finn. No shadows." Philby was slipping into Professor Philby mode.

"Finn's a hologram," Willa said. "A projection."

"Exactly!" Philby said.

"And why is this news?" Maybeck asked. "We know DHIs don't throw shadows."

"Look. Watch." Philby played the video. There was no sound. The dragon reared back, opened his mouth, and then fell as Charlene speared his heel. The column of fire erupted from his open mouth. Wayne burned up.

Everyone looked away from the screen at once.

"That's not fair!" Finn complained. "I do not want to see that again!"

"You've got to look, Finn. You all have to look. Not at Wayne, but behind him." Philby replayed the video.

"I don't believe it," whispered Finn in a ghostly voice.

"That's not possible," said Charlene.

Maybeck spoke. "It's got to be too much light.

Some kind of optical illusion. A bad angle or something."

"I'm not seeing what you all are seeing," Amanda complained.

"There's no shadow," Jess said. "Wayne's not casting a shadow."

"Because it isn't Wayne," Philby said. "He's a hologram."

"He's alive!" Finn's voice cracked. "He made himself into one of us. A DHI!"

"A Kingdom Keeper!" said Willa.

63

"WE ARE SO STUPID," Philby said.

"Speak for yourself," Maybeck fired back at him.

"Willa," Philby directed, "a quick review of our history with the Overtakers."

Willa scratched her hologram head and squinted. "Well, first they tried to rewrite the magic in the Magic Kingdom, and we stopped them. Wayne helped us. Helped us a lot. Amanda realized Maleficent had put Jess under a spell. Finn broke the spell. Then the Overtakers kidnapped Jess. We think Maleficent is afraid of Jess's ability to see the future, to anticipate Maleficent's next move. They hid Jess in Animal Kingdom, and we found her. Next, Wayne goes missing. That's why we're here. But we started in Epcot because everything pointed to him being in Epcot. Seems like a week ago, but that was just yesterday. You and Maybeck found Odin's sword. Amanda and I heard Chef and Mabel talking about putting Chernabog in a crate. Something like that. We're not really sure. The Overtakers were using the Fantasmic! show to hide in plain sight. All those characters belong there. No one would question seeing them there. They were using Fantasmic! as a base. Like a base for operations. We've now stopped that. It will much harder for them to hide. We're closer to ending them once and for all."

"So where's Wayne?" Philby asked. It was a test. Philby clearly knew the answer.

Silence. Everyone was deep in thought.

"Somewhere in Fantasmic!" Finn said. "It was their hideout. They would have kept Wayne close."

Philby smiled. "Being locked up in Fantasmic! meant he might be able to change the show there. To insert himself into the rehearsal as a DHI the way he did."

"But Charlene and I searched the entire stage, including backstage. The equipment rooms. Dressing rooms."

"Right," Philby said. "And I was in the control booth and I didn't see him."

"Then where?" Maybeck asked.

"Best place to hide is out in the open," Finn said, quoting Wayne.

"Second best," Philby said, "is to keep moving."

"I don't understand," Jess said.

"The boats!" Amanda said. "No one checked the boats."

Philby's smile turned into an enormous grin. "We never checked the boats."

64

"*STEAMBOAT WILLIE*. Has to be." Willa pointed out the boat to the group. Their DHIs had passed through a wall to reach the area behind the stage—all but Philby, who embarrassed himself trying to climb over.

A small lagoon encircled the stage.

The show's barges and boats were tied up behind the mountainous stage.

"You see the wheel up top? In the show, who steers the *Steamboat Willie*?" Professor Philby again.

"Captain Mickey," Willa said.

"Gold star!" said Philby.

"You two can be annoying." It was hard to tell when Maybeck was joking.

"Will there be Overtakers?" Amanda spoke what everyone was thinking.

"No doubt," Philby said.

"Charlene will scout it," Finn said, assuming his role as leader. I owe this to Wayne, he thought. "I'll be with her. I can force my all-clear. That may help us. We work in pairs. Amanda and Maybeck will follow if I give the sign. Amanda, we may need you to push the Overtakers." He wasn't going to mention that even as a DHI, Maybeck was the strongest. "There's a thick electrical cord running from the dock to the boat. Did everybody see that? Philby and Willa will disable the power. Cutting the power will cut any lights on the boat. That could help us. Jess is our scout. If you see trouble coming, shout and take off running. If things go bad, we'll meet after by the entrance to Pixar."

No one challenged Finn's plan or the assignments. He took this as a good sign. Tonight they were a complete team.

65

THE APPROACH TO THE lagoon behind Fantasmic! was hampered by a slow but steady rain. The coal colored sky swirled with mist and wind. Water on the lenses of DHI projectors blurred the holograms. Finn and the others looked more like ghosts than humans. In a burst of wet wind, holes appeared. The Keepers looked like Swiss cheese.

To increase their chances of success, the pairs stayed away from each other. Finn carried the sword. Charlene moved hunched over through the tall grass. She remained by Finn's side. Somewhere to their right, Philby and Willa snuck through the high grass. Maybeck and Amanda would draw near but await Finn's signal. Jess would watch it all.

"How many guards, do you think?" Charlene asked.

"No idea." Finn had already thought through this. "With what happened earlier, they won't dare try to move him tonight. But they'll move him as soon as possible. I'm guessing they might have had a guard on deck, but not tonight. Too risky. Park Security will be all over the place."

"So one or two below," she said.

"Yeah."

"Which characters?"

"That's important."

They were close now. Finn signaled for Charlene to stop. They kneeled in the grass, sweeping their eyes across the back of the show.

Charlene whispered, "I think it could be Jafar, or the palace guards in Aladdin. You?"

"I guess we'll find out."

They crawled on hands and knees. The grass passed through their holograms, unwavering. If anyone were watching, that person wouldn't see so much as a twitch of movement beyond that caused by the weather.

They came upon several barges and, in their center, *Steamboat Willie.* A white paddleboat with several decks, the boat's wheel was housed in a small deck at the very top. Mickey stood there during the show. Other characters would wave to the audience either forward or aft, or to port, facing the amphitheater. Those decks stood empty. There was a creepy feeling hanging in the air.

"You remember the plan?" Finn whispered.

"You have the sword. I don't. My DHI can go where yours can't. I remember."

"No heroics," Finn said. "We work as a team, Charlie."

"I said I remember the plan."

"Don't get mad at me. I'm trying to look out for you," Finn said.

"I'm a girl, Finn. I'm not dumb. I don't go back on what I agree to. Stop treating me like a baby."

"I didn't mean to. You're stronger than me. Faster. I didn't mean anything like that."

"Good. Then let's both stick to the plan, and maybe things will work out."

"Agreed."

All because of the sword, Finn held back to watch Charlene reach out, grab hold of a line connected to the steamboat, and swing her hologram through the boat's hull. She disappeared. Finn started counting to twenty.

66

THE BACK OF THE BOAT was as dark as Space Mountain. Nearly in DHI shadow, Charlene's hologram glowed as faint as a single candle. She looked more ghost than hologram. Studying her own arm and hand, she wondered if she might take advantage of her appearance.

She started counting down from twenty.

Finn had been right—this area of the boat held the engine. No one was in here. She generated just enough light to be able to guide her way through the heavy equipment to reach a small door. Rather than open the door and risk making noise, Charlene poked the head of her hologram through the door. She looked right, left, and drew back into the engine room. A row of dim lights lit the passageway. They mounted to the wall. No reason to have lights on unless someone was down here. Wayne?

Fourteen . . . thirteen . . .

If she didn't quickly get topside, Finn was going to come "rescue" her. *Boys!*

Again, she stuck her hologram head through the

door. Again, she looked around. Stepping into the passageway, she moved toward the lantern. An exit sign hung over the door just before the lantern.

She hurried. Reaching the exit, she found the door propped open with a paint can. She ducked inside the stairwell. Metal stairs painted white. Rising steeply. An open door. The night sky.

Eight . . . seven . . .

A flat shadow against that door.

Finn was a hologram. Holograms didn't cast shadows, so it wasn't Finn.

Her back to the handrail, Charlene carefully climbed the steep stairs.

Four . . . three . . .

Finn would ruin everything if he came charging onto the boat. She was one step from the open doorway when the shadow was swallowed by darkness. Beneath her, the light from the passageway failed as well.

Maybeck and Willa had cut the power line to the boat! Now closer to outside, her hologram looked less ghostly. She stepped higher.

Titans!

It looked like an alien skeleton made out of rock or metal. Pointed spikes rose from its shoulders and body. The spikes looked like icicles. Its long, ungainly legs were pipes. Ribs like coat hangers. Next to him was a blob of clay with two eyes. It was roughly the color of burned toast.

The head of the clay blob jiggled slightly. It took Charlene a fraction of a second to realize Finn's blade had sliced clean through the Titan. It took a step. Its head fell onto the ship deck with a thud.

The skeleton Titan blocked Finn's next attempt. Finn's sword clanged as it struck the Titan's forearm. The thing took a swing at Finn, who blocked the blow with his sword. The Titan stood at least a foot taller than Finn. Its arms were longer than Finn's. The Titan's next blow was a fist aimed at Finn's head. Charlene wasn't about to trust that Finn was pure hologram. If he wasn't, the Titan was about to break Finn's chin. Maybe his neck.

Charlene reached from behind and took the Titan by the arm. As the creature followed through, Charlene's grip spun him. Half the Titan swept through Charlene's hologram. The Titan's mouth was a large black hole. Above it, slanted slits served as eyes. The thing looked completely freaked!

With Charlene's hand hooked around the Titan's forearm, she got scared. Her hologram firmed, no longer all-clear.

Finn swung the sword. He cut off the Titan's arm. The Titan looked down as if he couldn't believe what had happened. Neither could Finn. Odin's sword had magical powers. Unreal strength.

Charlene was holding on to the severed arm. She dropped it and the arm banged to the deck.

Charlene signaled Finn to move toward her. She jumped to a spot immediately behind the Titan.

Finn swung the sword. The Titan backed up. One step. Two steps. Finn kept swinging. The Titan did not put his one good arm in the way of the sword. He jumped back when Finn shoved the tip of the sword at his ribs.

Four steps. Five.

Charlene dropped to hands and knees.

Finn understood. He took another strong lunge at the Titan with the sword outthrust. Hades's servant banged into the kneeling Charlene, waved his one good arm to try to regain his balance, and fell over the side.

Finn and Charlene rushed to watch as the lagoon's water boiled. A bubbling, steaming circle in the water spit and gurgled. The bubbles grew smaller. The boiling stopped.

Finn was dumbfounded. "How did you know to do that?"

"Jafar becomes a genie in the show. The genie summons Hades."

"Spirits from the dead."

"Exactly. From down there! The underworld. But how do you kill what's already dead?"

"Brilliant!" Finn said.

"The underworld is all fire. What puts out fire? Water. It's obvious."

"It wasn't to me," Finn admitted. "What about below?"

"Lights in the passageway," she said. "Someone's down there, or maybe these were the only two."

"I wouldn't count on that." Finn was looking at the open doorway. "Why didn't they come up when the power went out?"

"If anyone's down there, they'll stay close to Wayne."

"One of us draws them out," Finn said. "The other walks through walls and finds Wayne."

"Sounds right."

"I'll take the Titans. You find Wayne and defend him."

"I don't mean to be a problem maker, but listen, Finn, the Titans don't act on their own."

"They have a boss."

"They do."

"Hades."

"Not a nice boss," she said.

"I have the sword," he said, reminding her.

"He's the master of all death, Lord of the Underworld. Your sword may not bother him. What then?"

Finn looked up. A dozen pipes, all painted white and carrying small labels, ran overhead the full length of the passageway. "We improvise."

67

AMANDA HEARD IT BEFORE Maybeck. Having just unplugged the thick power cord leading to the steamboat, Maybeck was enjoying a self-satisfied moment. Maybeck was Maybeck's biggest fan.

"You see that? We did it!" he said proudly.

"Look behind us, Terry." Amanda's voice quavered.

As Maybeck turned his head his body went rigid. Several dozen purple slits were running toward him and Amanda. It took him a moment to realize the slits were eyes.

"I know those eyes," he murmured. "Who are they? What are they from?"

"Legion of Loa. Dr. Facilier's Friends on the Other Side."

"Evil spirits!" Maybeck's voice cracked.

"Dead spirits. Basically cute zombies."

Maybeck tightened his lips and sent forth a shrill whistle.

Amanda was horrified. "Why don't you just stand up, wave, and tell them where we are?"

"They aren't after us, Amanda. They're headed for the steamboat."

"Oh, my gosh!"

"We need Philby and Willa's help."

"To do what?"

Philby and Willa were seen running hunched over in the direction of Amanda and Maybeck.

The Legion of Loa had spread out side by side. There had to be twenty of the death spirits. They were blobby things with vivid purple slits for eyes. They were running.

"Grab the other end," Maybeck said, ordering Amanda.

"What end?"

"The power line. The extension cord. The end down by the water. I've got this end."

Amanda ran off.

Maybeck tried to judge the speed of the death spirits against the quickness of Philby and Willa. It was going to be a close race, but the spirits were going to win. That would be bad. He released a second whistle, this one softer.

Amanda, approaching where land met water, glanced back.

Maybeck stood and thrust both arms out. Amanda

stopped abruptly. She turned around, nodded at Maybeck, and straightened her posture. Maybeck dropped to his knees and then lay flat on the ground. He knew what came next.

Just as he planted himself into the ground, the grasses around him bent sharply behind a ferocious wind. Amanda had *pushed* in the direction of the oncoming spirits. For a brief few seconds it felt like a hurricane had struck. The wind stopped.

Maybeck sat up.

The spirits were scattered. All had lost their footing. A few struggled to stand.

Philby and Willa slid to a stop.

"Legion of Loa!" Philby said. He knew way too much.

"You help Amanda. Willa's with me," Maybeck said. He reached down and picked up the thick, heavy electric cable. "Tug-o-war," he said.

"Got it!" Philby ran toward the water.

"On our butts," Maybeck told Willa. "Heels planted."

"I've played this game before." Willa crouched in front of Maybeck and took the cable in both hands. Maybeck held the identical posture behind her.

"It's heavy. So we wait until Philby and Amanda are ready, and the purple slits are right here."

"Understood."

The various forces came into play. The eyes of the fallen death spirits reappeared. They organized and began running once again. In the distance, down by the water, Amanda and Philby struggled with the heavy power cable. They managed to drag it until they reached a spot directly across from Willa and Maybeck, still crouching, still holding on to their end. Amanda and Philby were at least twenty yards away, just glowing hologram specks.

The Friends from the Other Side charged now, coming like the cavalry. They were silent, dark fleshy blobs with frowns and melted expressions. The closer they drew, the uglier they became. Willa looked away.

"Stay ready," Maybeck whispered.

She nodded.

The evil spirits could be heard now. They sounded like a fall wind blowing swirling dry leaves. Willa's hologram had goose bumps. She had lost all-clear.

The things were bigger than they'd appeared at a distance. Some stood three or four feet tall. Others were as tall as grown-ups.

Maybeck whistled. He and Willa half stood, and, pulling, leaning, tightened the cable. Amanda and Philby did the same from their end. The heavy cable rose off the ground just as the spirits arrived.

It took all of their strength to hold the cable fast. The spirits hit the cable as a group. They tripped and rolled. They made the strangest of sounds—like wounded cats. They tumbled, flailed and rolled into the water. All of them. Nearly at once.

There was splashing and thrashing. The strange cat sound mixed with the bubbling of water. All four Keepers looked away, unable to watch.

"How did you know to do that?" Willa asked Maybeck. "You beat them!"

"I had to take a chance," Maybeck answered. "I asked myself: Even if an evil spirit could fly, when would it have learned to swim?"

68

FINN DIDN'T NEED TO LEAN his hologram head through the door in the steamboat's lower passageway. He didn't need to inspect every door in the long line of doors. He didn't need to press his ear to the various doors and listen intently for sounds from the other side. Disney kept its Parks sparkling clean. That included the boats behind Fantasmic! Boats like the *Steamboat Willie*. The walls were painted a pristine white; the passageway floors, a glistening marine gray. In front of one door, and one door only, a line of muddy shoe prints led from the bottom of the stairs.

Finn motioned to Charlene. She carefully moved to the next door down—a different room—walked through the wall, and disappeared.

Finn closed his eyes. He summoned a pure darkness, like standing in an underground tunnel. He looked for a bright speck of light at the end of the tunnel. He felt his entire body flood with heat and the unsettling feeling of a limb falling asleep. He was all-clear.

He threw open the door.

Any Kingdom Keeper knew the difference between a Disney film character, a Park Cast Member character, and the real thing.

Hades was enormous. Blisteringly hot even from a distance. His skin was gray, his eyes, green. His sharply pointed teeth fit together like a jack-o'-lantern's. Finn needed a change of underwear. He might have been all-clear but was no longer all clean.

"Ah hah," Hades said, his voice like a door with rusted hinges. He seemed happy to see Finn. Behind the Lord of the Dead, Wayne was tied to a metal chair. He shook his head. His concerned eyes said, *No!*

A trap! Finn thought he understood Wayne's shaking head. Hades, perhaps working with Maleficent and the other Overtakers, had taken Wayne to lure Finn and the Keepers.

"Welcome, Child of Light." Hades's voice was more growl than speech, more menace than welcome. Finn worked to maintain his state of all-clear.

The demon lifted his arm, twisted his hand like he was opening a doorknob.

Finn felt a swirl of heat overwhelm him. Hades had cast a spell. Finn squinted, pictured the pinprick of light at the end of the tunnel. The heat cooled. The spell had missed.

Hades pulled his hand toward himself. He expected

to drag Finn closer. Finn's DHI didn't move. The grin on the face of Hades became a snarl.

"You want to play with Hades?"

"You will release Wayne, or I will dispatch you." Finn hoisted the sword in front of his own face.

"Do you really think a toy knife will have any effect on me?"

"No, I don't," Finn answered, confusing Hades. "But this is not a 'toy knife.' This is Odin's sword. Odin, the god of wisdom, poetry, death, and magic."

The demon's eyes flared.

"Care for a bite?" Finn said, swinging the blade.

"No, Finn!" Wayne called, his mouth gagged, his words muddled.

An angry Hades lifted both arms. Another spell was coming. Finn braced for it. Twice the force. Twice the rage in the demon's eyes. His words came out slowly, like he was chewing them. "You and yours have been a thorn in our side, young man. One should not undertake a purpose greater than one's ability to execute it. Poor judgment, that. Bad form. Ambition is one's downfall. Acceptance of one's role in life gets the job done. You have overstepped your place. You will join me now. You and yours. I have a place for you. A forever place. Some call it the Underworld. It is in fact so much more than that. I like to call it Crispy Dreams."

Hades threw his long arms forward. Gray hands. Sharpened fingernails. The moment it happened Finn understood he wouldn't escape the demon's power this time. It was no contest. Try as he had, Finn couldn't maintain his all-clear. Fear had won out. Hades had won.

Two legs appeared, head height. One plunged behind Hades's head, the other, bent at the knee, choked the demon. Charlene had slipped through the side wall and had managed some kind of gymnastics or a martial arts move. Her momentum carried Hades over, like a giant crane tipping. Whatever spell he threw struck the room's metal wall. The white paint blistered and turned black. It stunk. The metal, along with the burned paint, turned into a green goo and sank toward the floor.

Hades grabbed for Charlene's leg that had him in a chokehold. Finn felt the sword in his hand grow cold. He looked up again at the overhead pipes.

"Let him go, Charlie!"

"What? No!"

"Let him go. I want him for myself."

"No!"

"Now! Free Wayne! Get him to safety."

Hades struggled.

"I can't let you do this!" Charlene was screaming.

"Let . . . him . . . go!"

Charlene released her hold on Hades. She rolled away toward Wayne.

A furious Hades, an embarrassed Hades, pulled himself up to standing and marched out into the hallway. "You impertinent boy. You should not have done that. Never release that which you possess."

Finn needed the demon to take one more step. "I notice you stand away from Odin's sword. Scared, are we?"

"Brazen of you. You will discover the infinity of my powers once you are finally and firmly dead." He lifted but a single finger as he stepped forward. "Say good night, Child of Light."

Finn swung the sword overhead and sliced open the pipe marked COOLANT. A turquoise gas spewed out the end. It turned white and frosty as it impaled Hades. It looked to be an element somewhere between foam and ice. The beast released a ghastly shriek. Finn hoisted the sword and sank the sharpened tip into the demon's chest. It was like stabbing a chunk of ice.

Hades collapsed and broke into a thousand pieces, all smoking like dry ice.

"He will reassemble!" Wayne called. Charlene had untied Wayne and helped him to his feet. "Nothing can kill the Lord of the Underworld. You have slowed him, but you have not stopped him. We must hurry!"

As Wayne said this, several of the broken pieces on the floor moved and found others. Finn watched as the pieces turned to fit together like a jigsaw puzzle.

He tiptoed through the pieces. With Charlene holding one arm and Finn the other, they helped Wayne up the ladderway and off the boat.

Fresh air, at last.

69

PHILBY'S ONLY CONVERSATION with Wayne had been brief. Wayne had spoken in a whisper, not out of weakness, but in the interest of secrecy.

"There is more going on than meets the eye. It's much bigger than you think."

"What Amanda and Willa heard in France?"

"A part of it, yes. Present your evidence to the Imagineers. They will believe you. There will be security video. I am sure of it."

"Maleficent, Chernabog, and Hades. All Overtakers, all working together."

"It's much bigger than we knew."

The paramedics had approached. The conversation had stopped as the medics whisked Wayne away and into an ambulance.

70

Days blended into weeks. Philby used his control of the hologram software to prevent any Keeper from crossing over.

Finn turned in his cell phone and computer as part of his punishment. It would be a month or more before his parents would give him back some of his freedoms. Despite the discipline, he and his mom would lock eyes every so often. At the dinner table. Across the kitchen. Finn saw joy in her eyes. He smiled back at her. It was more than just him being safe. It was her way to tell him that she understood now. She'd witnessed the Keepers in action.

School was school: *b o r i n g*. Except at lunch when Amanda would slide onto the bench next to him. Sometimes he would see something in her eyes as well. Though he didn't understand it, he liked it. He would fight back a smile for her as well.

One particular lunch, one he wouldn't soon forget, she sat extremely close to him. She whispered, speaking without looking at him.

"I don't know how to explain this," she said.

"Try."

"I'm a Fairlie," she said.

"I think we've established that."

"We Fairlies all have special . . . abilities."

"Powers," he said.

"We don't think of them that way. But okay. Whatever. We have them. What I'm able to do is to *push*. To levitate. To move things away from me."

He swallowed dryly. "You mean me."

"Almost anything I want to."

"What if I don't want to be pushed away? Just because you're good at something," he said, "doesn't mean it has to own you. There are people that let that happen, and there are people that don't. It's a choice, not a prison sentence."

"That makes it sound easier than it is."

"Let me put it this way: You can push me away all you want, but I'm like a human yo-yo. I'm going to come right back at you."

"It's what I do. I pushed my family away without meaning to—or I wouldn't be without them."

"You don't know that. You don't know what happened to them."

"I can imagine."

"Wayne taught us to imagine the good, Amanda. It is an option. You know? Seriously."

She sighed, deeply frustrated.

He placed his hand onto hers. Hers was icy cold. His, phenomenally warm.

"A human yo-yo," he repeated. He won a smile from her.

"You're Kingdom Keepers now. You and Jess both are. You know that, right?"

She nodded.

"There are ways we do things," he said. "As a group. For each other. We always team up. No one ever goes alone."

She looked totally stressed out.

"No one ever goes alone," he repeated. "I'll tell you something: I don't like girls. But I like you. I don't care about girls, but I care about you, and Willa, and Jess, and Charlene, too. Nothing bad is ever going to happen to any of you. That's just the way it is. You and Jess are part of that now. You can't get out of it. No one ever goes alone."

"Are you going to eat that?" she asked, pointing to something that might have once been pineapple. It looked like a kitchen sponge.

"Not now, not ever," he said. "Go for it."

She reached over and snagged it and ate it in two bites.

"Well, if it isn't Thin Wit-less!" growled the voice of

Greg Luowski. He carried a string of zits from his nose all the way over to his ear. Mike Horton stood to the side and slightly behind him.

"And the evil witch," Luowski added. "Blown any houses off-course lately?"

"Take a hike, Luowski," Finn said.

"You and me, we've got unfinished business."

"Mike," Finn said, "I thought you were going to get him a better writer?"

Horton tried to keep the grin off his face.

Luowski said, "Your girly-friend isn't always going to be around, Whitman. Don't you think it's kind of spineless to need a girl to do your fighting for you?"

"Sticks and stones, Luowski. You know I'm not going to fight you. You're a cretin. And if you don't know what that means, look it up."

"I'm coming for you, Whitman."

"Get in line," Finn said. "You and everyone else."

"Mike," Amanda said to Horton, "do me a favor and get Greg out of here before there's trouble."

Horton led Luowski away. Luowski tried to look like he wanted to hang around, but Finn knew better. Amanda had him and half the school scared.

"You realize we're outcasts?" Finn said.

"Yes. I've been one my whole life. It's not so bad really. You get used to it."

"I'm working on it."

"I can help you," she said.

"I'd like that, I think. But remember I don't like girls."

"Yes. So you said."

"Just so we're clear on that."

"Perfectly."

71

SIX WEEKS AFTER Wayne's rescue, DHIs of the Keepers along with Amanda and Jess were sitting in a long line. They were the only seven souls in all of Fantasmic! Philby had arranged with Wayne to cross them over this one time.

They'd spent nearly all their time in Star Wars: Galaxy's Edge. The entire area all to themselves. They had ridden the rides a dozen times. Best night ever.

"Can you imagine," the professor said, "if the *Millennium Falcon* came 'alive' the same way other rides have come alive for us?"

"We'd end up in space?" Willa said.

"I think we might."

"I'm down with that," Maybeck said. "I get to fly it. I'm definitely our Han Solo."

"More like Chewbacca," Charlene said, teasing him.

"We ought to cross over again and try it."

"Jess the adventurer! Who knew?" Amanda said, laughing.

"This Park is definitely troubled," Jess said.

"Yes," Finn said. "I feel it, too."

"We all feel it," Willa said.

"We're not done here." Philby could sound more serious than any of them. Maybe all of them combined. "There's the Chernabog thing. Hades being involved. The fact that they're after Finn, or all of us."

"At least we've got Wayne." Amanda yawned.

It caught on. Several yawned in succession. "And Wanda," Philby said. "She's with us now."

"Do you think there will ever be more of us?" Charlene asked. "A new version of us, or maybe they'll just shut us down and never allow us to be holograms ever again?"

"I'm taking precautions against that," Philby said.

It sent shivers down Finn. "As in?"

"Modeling their computer server. It's a work in progress. It'll take time. But I hope to have our own DHI projection server someday."

"That's open rebellion!" Finn said.

"It's self-preservation," Philby said. "We have work to do. We're a team."

"We're the freakin' Kingdom Keepers," Maybeck said.

"If Amanda and I don't wake up in our beds, Ms. Nash will call an ambulance."

"My mom will ground me for eternity," Willa said.

"Okay," Finn said. He opened his hand, revealing

the Return fob. "But we all agree we're going to do whatever it takes to help Wayne shut down the Overtakers and keep the Parks safe. Yes?"

Some nodded. Others answered, "Yes."

"Okay then," Finn said. "One for all, and all of that."

He pushed the button.

ACKNOWLEDGMENTS 2010

Thanks to Nancy Litzinger Zastrow for running my office. To Amy Berkower, Dan Conaway, and, especially, Genevieve Gange-Hawes—all of Writers House, New York. Also to Matthew Snyder, of CAA.

At Disney Book Group I want to thank Wendy Lefkon, Jennifer Levine, Nellie Kurtzman, Frankie Lobono, Jessica Ward, and the whole publishing team for all the help on these projects.

The Kingdom Keepers books wouldn't exist without the on-site research, and this time around (Epcot and Disney's Hollywood Studios) the research wouldn't have happened without the dedication and time from all of the following: Alex Wright, Jason Grandt and Debra Wren, Pete Glim, Jeff Terry, Brian Ripley, Tom Devlin, Rachel at Soarin', and Lorraine and Philip at the Engineering Base.

Thanks to everyone for keeping the magic alive.

—*Ridley Pearson*
January 2010
St. Louis

Get a sneak peek of Ridley Pearson's new Kingdom Keepers book
Inheritance

Coming March 2021

1

Eli Whitman lifted his hands and screamed. He was sitting in the front row of Animal Kingdom's roller coaster, Expedition Everest. The thing was older than his parents! He could imagine the views from outside. Giraffe and hippos in the Kilimanjaro Safari. White seagulls perched atop the Tree of Life.

His friends cried out as the roller coaster dove. Parents weren't on the ride. Fine with him. At twelve and thirteen, he and his friends didn't need hand-holding.

As the roller coaster stopped, Eli had a brief view of Pandora, an attraction more than twenty years old. The Siberian Forest Climb and the Great Barrier Reach had opened two years earlier. That had been Animal Kingdom's fortieth birthday. Other kids might have gone there for a birthday party. Not Eli. Expedition Everest was his favorite. And this was, after all, his birthday party.

Animal Kingdom was super crowded. Tomorrow there would be a total solar eclipse. The Disney Parks had special shows planned, including a Star Wars Sky Search.

When the roller coaster entered the double loop, Marie-Claire grabbed Eli's hand. She squeezed and held on tight. That made it the best day-before-his-birthday ever.

When he got off the ride, he stopped at the show wall to see a video of himself on the ride. The other kids looked strong or pretty. He saw himself as boring-looking. Freckles. Brown hair. Darkish skin. (His mother was part Asian; his father, Caucasian.) Eli didn't think of himself as good-looking. In the video, the wind pushed back his hair. It gave away a secret: He kept his hair long to hide his gigantic ears.

The July air felt hot and damp. He was sweaty. Jungle trees and vines lined the path back toward the Monkey Temple. It was a place Eli liked to stop and watch for a while. He and Marie-Claire and a few other friends did just that. The sound of laughter filled the air. *Happy birthday*, he thought.

The group explored the rock canyons leading to Harambe. His parents had once tried to explain what the park had looked like back in 2020. But it was impossible for Eli not to see the solar holograms of the Disney Cast Members—Solograms—moving around throughout the park. He knew the hover carts were new. And so were attractions like Lock Nest Nessie that he counted as favorites.

He knew he was lucky. Not everyone got to live in a place like Epcot's CommuniTree. He had things others didn't. But he also wanted to travel more, like his parents did. They were currently riding the Boring Hyperloop from Atlanta to Los Angeles. Instead of being with them, he was in the park. His parents listened; they just didn't seem to ever hear him.

Maybe things would change tomorrow. Thirteen had to be better than twelve.

"Did you know that people in India don't eat during a solar eclipse because they think any food would be poisoned?" At ten, Lily Perkins was too young to hang out with sixth and seventh graders. There were unwritten rules about such things. But she was funny and smart, and she always made him feel better. To Eli, that was the definition of a good friend, and so he'd invited her.

"I did not," he admitted.

"In some cultures, pregnant women stay indoors during an eclipse." Her eye color matched her straight hair perfectly—brown with flecks of highlight in both. Her hair was very fine, and hung past her shoulders. She smiled for Eli and giggled, sounding like a complaining squirrel.

"Because?" he asked.

"Superstition." Lily wore a light-blue T-neck pullover, dandelion-yellow baggy cropped pants, and aquamarine retro-Moana flip-flops.

Eli's parents listened to extremely old music, including a singer named Stevie Wonder who'd written a pretty good song, "Superstitious." The music started swirling in Eli's head and he felt his foot tapping. *Ver-y super-sti-tious.* He loved music. Any kind. But he didn't tell his friends that. So-called friends judged you on all kinds of stuff that shouldn't matter. He'd learned that the hard way.

"It's not all scary," Lily said. Thing about Lily: if you let her get going, it was hard to stop her.

"Is that so?" An only child, Eli was really nice to other kids, especially younger girls, whom he saw as little sisters. Like little Lily. Lily was the best, funniest, most unexpected creature on the planet.

"In Italy, some people think that flowers planted during a solar eclipse turn out more colorful than others. So, what do you think it means when a boy's thirteenth birthday is on the solar eclipse?"

"I dunno," Eli said, nervously.

"Maybe you'll grow a beard or something."

"Doubtful." Eli longed for the day he would start shaving.

"Maybe you'll start to age faster than everyone else your age."

"Now you're just being creepy," Eli said.

"Or find a princess." She giggled. "Other than Marie-Claire."

Eli swung to hit her playfully, but Lily saw and dodged the hit. Marie-Claire, who was French like her single mom, had transitioned from being Eli's lab partner, to friend, to someone he now regularly texted with. The more they texted, the more Eli had trouble not texting her back. It was becoming a habit. If someone like little Lily had noticed, he had big problems.

"You know what I think?" Lily said.

"I'm not sure I want to." Eli hoped she would stop.

"I think you only wanted to ride Expedition Everest so Marie-Claire would freak out and hold your hand in the dark."

"Are you a mind-reader?"

"Not exactly," Lily said sheepishly. "Kinda close, though." She giggled nervously.

Something about the way she said that interested Eli. He made a mental note to ask her more later.

"Keep that to yourself, will you, Lily?"

She ran off, skipping like a six-year-old. Eli smiled.